"We Won't Let A Girl Ride!"

The leader of the delegation of jockeys averted his eyes from Julie's as he spoke, but there was no wavering in his voice. The jockeys would boycott the big race rather than let Julie Jefferson ride as a jockey against them.

Julie heard those words like the voice of doom itself. After a cruel beating by a bad rider, Bonnie would run well only for her. Julie had defied all prejudices to win her jockey's license—and now this.

Should she defy the jockeys and ruin the entire race? Should she let another ride Bonnie and risk a humiliating defeat? Or was there another last desperate card she could play?

JULIE HAD TO DECIDE FAST—FOR THE CLOCK WAS RUNNING OUT . . .

Other SIGNET Titles You Will Enjoy

☐ **THE SWEET RUNNING FILLY by Pat Johnson and Barbara Van Tuyl.** A sympathetic and loving story of horses based on a real incident in the racing world. (#T4848—75¢)

☐ **TWINK by John Neufeld.** A gutsy, sometimes real tale of a girl with cerebral palsy who could have been forgotten, and wasn't, and how love and touching and caring made the difference in the face of an almost overwhelming physical handicap. (#T4819—75¢)

☐ **LINDA'S HOMECOMING by Phyllis A. Whitney.** A glowing novel of the joy and pain of growing up— from one of America's most beloved storytellers. Young and old alike will find a friend in Linda. (#T4793—75¢)

☐ **LISA BRIGHT AND DARK by John Neufeld.** Lisa is slowly going mad but her symptoms, even an attempted suicide, fail to alert her parents or teachers to her illness. She finds compassion only from three girlfriends who band together to provide what they call "group therapy." (#T4387—75¢)

A Horse Called Bonnie

By PAT JOHNSON
And
BARBARA van TUYL

A SIGNET BOOK from
NEW AMERICAN LIBRARY
TIMES MIRROR

THIRD PRINTING

 SIGNET TRADEMARK REG. U.S. PAT. OFF. AND FOREIGN COUNTRIES
REGISTERED TRADEMARK—MARCA REGISTRADA
HECHO EN CHICAGO, U.S.A.

SIGNET, SIGNET CLASSICS, SIGNETTE, MENTOR AND PLUME
BOOKS *are published by The New American Library, Inc.,
1301 Avenue of the Americas, New York, New York 10019*

First Printing, December, 1971.

PRINTED IN THE UNITED STATES OF AMERICA

A Horse Called Bonnie

Prologue

The Registrar
The Jockey Club
300 Park Avenue
New York, N.Y.

Dear Sir:

Four hundred thousand dollars is rather an extra-ordinary price for any horse. I am sure, therefore, that you will remember last year's Fasig-Tipton auction sales at Saratoga, when, because of her excellent bloodlines, I paid that amount for a yearling filly by Bold Ruler out of Starcrossed. She was registered under the name of Star Princess. However, she is not registered under that name now.

Let me explain this paradox, as briefly as possible.

My trainer, Alex Homer, at the time that Star Princess came under his control, conceived a criminal plot by which he hoped to obtain her for himself. With the aid of one Zeke Matthews, who was barred from racing several years ago for drugging a horse, he set out to find a double for Star Princess. This was fairly easy, as she is a solid rich bay without markings; they soon discovered an almost identical Thoroughbred of her age on a Kentucky farm. Buying this filly, they had her illegally tattooed with the lip number (673954) of Star Princess. Then they substituted her for my horse.

The original filly was hidden on a farm that had been rented by Matthews. The plot was to wait until the look-alike horse, or ringer, had proved herself an incurable lemon, and then to persuade me to salvage what I could by entering her in a claiming race. Homer would buy her, perform what you might call a "double-ringer ceremony" by resubstituting the genuine Bold Ruler filly, who would then begin to win races and eventually make these two villains rich; and this scheme might have worked out perfectly except for the nervousness of Zeke Matthews.

Alone on his rented farm with the fantastically valuable horse, he began to see spies and policemen in every shadow. The fact that if he were discovered, he could not implicate Alex Homer in the plot by any means that could be proved in court added to his ever-increasing fear. At last he took the filly to Ohio and gave her to a man named Samuel Spire, who runs a kind of junk yard and cheap livestock market. Spire was to destroy her and hide the remains. Matthews did not, of course, tell Homer about this, but disappeared into the countryside. He intended to wait until Homer was ready to put the plan into execution, and then to blackmail him for all the trade would bear, after which he would vanish for good, leaving Homer with a practically worthless filly of unknown breeding.

Now, however, thanks to the greed and the essential kindheartedness of the man Spire, Zeke Matthews was doublecrossed, even as he had doublecrossed Alex Homer. For Spire did not kill Star Princess, but sold her to a girl named Julie Jefferson; she was then named "Bonnie," by which name I will refer to her hereafter.

Naturally, Miss Jefferson had no knowledge of the filly's history. The animal being in a bad way, underfed and injured, she devoted her time to bringing it back to health for a month or more. Bonnie was kept at the St. Clair breeding farm, where her new owner worked as an assistant trainer under Montgomery Everett and his father Will Everett, whose name will be familiar to you as an old and honored one in racing circles.

The ringer had then been racing, and finishing out

of the money, long enough to earn the scornful title of "The Deepwater Lemon," my farm being known as Deepwater. You may imagine my disgust with what I believed to be a $400,000 bit of horseflesh. Homer's conspiracy would doubtless have made him a wealthy man had not Matthews turned chicken; and it would have cost me a fortune had not Julie Jefferson been a thoroughly honest and admirably tenacious young lady.

In October she discovered that Bonnie could run. Tracing her by the tattooed registration number on her lip, Miss Jefferson became convinced that her Bonnie was the real Bold Ruler filly. Although she believed she would lose the horse, which she had come to love very much, she nevertheless got in contact with me and told me the whole story; at least, as much as she then knew. I did not believe her. I did not know her then as well as I do now. Today I would believe Julie Jefferson if she told me that she had found a colt whose pedigree went straight back to Pegasus and Babieca.

She and Monty Everett thereupon set out to prove that Bonnie was Star Princess, and that Star Princess (who was still gamely losing for me) was some little fly-by-night Thoroughbred from nowhere in particular. The two of them, getting mixed up with the criminal Matthews and later with my crooked trainer, Homer, were catapulted into a series of encounters and dangerous events that I can only call by the good old-fashioned name of "adventures." In the course of these, they proved their belief to be true, and uncovered the whole plot. Working with St. Clair's head groom, Stash Watkins, and later with Leon Pitt, who served as head stud groom for the late Monroe Bradley and has now come out of retirement to act as my foreman on Fieldstone Farm (which I am in process of buying), Miss Jefferson and Monty Everett effected the capture of Matthews and Homer, and saved both fillies from destruction, at considerable risk to their own lives. Matthews and Homer are in jail awaiting trial.

I will now retire the counterfeit Star Princess, I believe; although I will attempt to trace her proper breeding, just for the record—and out of curiosity. A telephone conversation today with your Racing Secretary has suggested that much confusion would result if Bonnie were raced under her own original name and number, which of course have the ringer's race record attached to them. So Miss Jefferson will come in on Thursday morning will all the necessary papers, photographs, and so forth, to establish a new registration number and name for Bonnie, née Star Princess.

Bonnie will race under the blue and white of Deepwater Farm, and eventually Miss Jefferson and I will share in the foals she produces after her retirement from the track; otherwise, she is Julie's horse. For Bonnie, after all, owes her life and her future career entirely to the bravery, honesty, and decency of this courageous girl.

I will appreciate anything you can do to expedite the new registration of the much-adventured Bonnie.

Sincerely,

Rollin L. Tolkov

"And you're Julie Jefferson," said the Jockey Club Steward for about the fourth time, shaking his head incredulously. "I expected a sort of Amazon, after this story," he went on, picking up Tolkov's letter from his desk. "Good heavens! You look about as tough as my own daughter, and she's just out of high school."

"So am I," said Julie, brushing back her long blond hair and smiling uncertainly. "Five months out, anyway."

"Well, my respects, Miss Jefferson. You certainly seem to have done the sport of kings a good turn, ferreting out those two bad apples and restoring a Bold Ruler filly to the track. We'll try to smooth the path for you all we can, but it's a complicated case, quite unlike anything we've had before, to my knowledge. Did you bring photographs of, uh, Bonnie?"

"About half a zillion," said Julie. "I mean, yes, a good many." She emptied one of the two manila envelopes onto the desk. "These are of Bonnie. We took them from every possible angle, I guess. And these are of Star Princess."

"Almost no difference between them, is there?"

"If you really know Bonnie you can spot her right

away. She's a very super horse," Julie said proudly. "Here's the application forms for her registration." Then she slid out the contents of the second envelope. "Affidavit from Leon Pitt that the scar on Bonnie's elbow is from a cut that he stitched up when she fell on a rock, when she was just a baby. Affidavit from a veterinarian that the scar's the same as Leon describes. Mr. T's affidavit—that is, Mr. Tolkov's—that Bonnie's the real thing, proved to his satisfaction. Here are the papers of Star Princess, you know, the *other* one: her race record and foal certificate, and a verification from the vet that she's tattooed with Bonnie's number. Affidavits from Stash Watkins, he was there when Zeke Matthews confessed the whole story to us; and from Max McGraw, of Kandahar Park, who was there too, you must know him, he's in charge of the stable area . . ."

"I believe I've met him, yes." The Steward smiled up at her. He was examining the application for registration, especially the diagrams. "No star, blaze, stripe, or snips?"

"No, she has no markings at all except for the tiny little scar, and that's hidden. She's a beautiful horse," Julie assured him fervently. "You ought to see her."

"Maybe I will. I expect a representative of the Jockey Club will have to take a look at both of them. We're professionally hard to convince of anything," he told her. "We have to be. We're the watchdogs of racing. It's up to us to keep everything straightforward."

Julie nodded. "I know. They're both at Deepwater Farm, in Kentucky. We work there, Monty and I. For Mr. T. Monty's his new trainer—that is, he will be when he passes the exam for his license—and I'm Monty's assistant. Monty's taking his New York trainer's exam now, because it's the toughest and then he'll take the Kentucky one, see? So anyway you can see both horses at Deepwater, and here's an affidavit from Sam Spire, swearing to the fact that Zeke Matthews gave him Bonnie to be put down; and here's the three names I'm submitting for her, in order of preference, and . . . and I guess that's all."

"Except that you're very anxious about the whole thing."

"Right."

"Well, try not to be," he said, looking at the three names. "It's complicated, and we're stern and tough, but we're fair. Hmm. Sunbonnet. Let's see." He picked up a book from his desk. "There are a quarter of a million names in this volume that you can't use; names of horses now alive, or gone less than fifteen years, or of course the great ones—you'd be amazed at how many people want to call their Thoroughbreds 'Whirla-way' or 'Seabiscuit'—no, there's no Sunbonnet. That's a good start. The Registrar will have to okay it, but I'd say you have a pretty good chance of your first choice being accepted, which is a rare thing."

"That would be lovely. Because she'll always be Bon-nie to me."

He read the names on the form. "Sunbonnet, Bon-nie Braes, Bonniebelle. We'll see. Thanks for bringing all this material in, Miss Jefferson. You'll be hearing from us."

Julie thanked him and left the premises, shaking slightly with timidity. She had faced angry criminals and been less afraid than she was at the complex official red tape that now surrounded her and her horse. It was considerably worse, she thought, than being back in school facing an algebra test. It was so appallingly grown-up and mysterious! She felt like a small and im-mature Alice at the entrance to a cold, heartless Won-derland. The Steward had been nice, but she'd been told so many stories of the intricate mazes of the Jockey Club's paperwork that she couldn't believe she was not setting out on a couple of months' worth of lec-tures, setbacks, and application-fillings.

When, several days later, Mr. Tolkov found her in the tack room and informed her happily that Bonnie was officially Sunbonnet, with the registration number 677820, she was so relieved that she swallowed a mouthful of cola the wrong way and had to be pounded on the back for two minutes before she stopped chok-ing. Then she laughed so hard, with relief and joy, that she gave herself a bad case of hiccoughs.

Chapter I

Deepwater Farm, which lies in the heart of the Blue-grass region of central Kentucky, is a large and beautiful spread of fertile land nearly five thousand acres in extent. When Rollin Tolkov decided, at the age of fifty, to shorten his sixteen-hour work day drastically, and put some of his numerous millions of dollars into a racing plant, he never intended to become one of the pillars of the turf—that is, one of the big breeders of Thoroughbred racers. He only wanted to buy and race stakes winners. However, as he never did anything in a small way, which is probably the main reason why he was a self-made millionaire, he had his agents look for the finest, largest farm available. This was Deepwater.

Deepwater got into his blood very quickly. He had always been fond of the track, and now he became obsessed with it from the other side; the spectator turned into the owner within about twenty-four hours, it seemed, and soon he began to plan a further career as a breeder of great stock. So after two years, during which he relinquished more and more of the control of his firm, Uni-Tea, that huge commercial complex, to the several junior partners, he purchased Fieldstone Farm, half an hour's easy drive from Deepwater, which was to be his breeding farm. Here he installed Leon Pitt as foreman. Leon had already put in forty years of his life on Fieldstone, ending as head stud groom; he was the best man possible for the job of managing the place.

Deepwater would always remain his true love, though, Tolkov thought as he walked briskly from the main house toward the biggest of the horse barns. He had even established an office here, from which a good deal of the business of Uni-Tea itself was now conducted. He did not like to be away from his horses too long; or from his beautiful farm, either.

From the distant road, a long blacktop driveway roamed through great fields of alfalfa, timothy, bluegrass and clover, from which the animals' hay would come. A quarter of a mile from the main house, the drive widened to become a parkway, lined with poplars and turf. It came in from the southwest past the one-mile track and turned due north to the steps of the Old South portico with its tall white pillars. The house was enormous. The main portion was 1895, and the two wings 1960. Tolkov's four-room office quarters were in the west wing, as well as the living quarters for his two secretaries; in the east wing, the farm manager and the maids and other servants had their rooms. Mr. T himself lived in solitary, sometimes rather lonely grandeur in the central pile.

Just to the west of the house was the gigantic horse barn, the principal one. It contained sixty stalls set back to back in two long rows separated down the center by an aisle, so that the compartments were grouped in four sets of fifteen each. The stalls were encircled by a very broad aisle, twice as large as the central one—in really bad weather the horses were worked up and down this aisle, which was wide enough for three of them going abreast—and the ends of each stall row were cut off catercornered, so that the aisle became a small imitation of an oval training track, around which the animals could jog slowly with no trouble. There were usually about fifty horses stabled in this great shed.

Also in this building was a room, the size of a couple of stalls, where medicines and hot and cold running water were available, as well as buckets, bandages, and numerous other necessities of animal and human life.

Twenty feet along a dirt road that led from the barn to the huge mile-round training track, a small building

housed the tack room, where saddles, bridles, and all
the other tack were kept on pegs and racks and stands;
here there was hot water too, and vending machines
for hungry grooms and thirsty exercise boys.

On west from the major shed was the trainers' cottage. Here Monty and Julie had taken up residence,
each in a large and pleasantly furnished room. The third
room was a kitchen-and-lounging place, and the fourth
was occupied, as it had been for a couple of years, by
Dan Gibson, a twenty-four-year-old exercise boy who
had hopes of being a trainer himself some day.

To the north of these buildings was a secondary horse
barn, used principally for housing lay-ups, temporary
cripples, and other ailing Thoroughbreds. Half a mile
to the east was the caretaker's cottage, near which sat a
number of sheds for tractors, farm equipment, and tools
and other paraphernalia for maintaining the farm.

Everywhere you looked there were fences; white-
board-fenced enclosures on both sides of the road, scat-
tered around both horse barns, along either edge of the
cinder track that led to the caretaker's place, and north-
ward almost to the wide shallow stream that meandered
down from the high meadows. The paddocks ranged
from large, for pasturing and exercising, to tiny, for
sunning only. Mr. T had no idea of their number. He
just knew there were enough.

In the northwestern section of Deepwater there were
some unexplored caverns of the sort typical of the
Bluegrass region. Here and there in the fertile, rich
loam stood small groves of walnut and sycamore trees,
in which lived possums, skunks, raccoons, woodchucks,
squirrels, and enough rabbits to populate the state of
Rhode Island. There was a trout stream near the south
border, as well as the shallow brook that separated the
northernmost paddocks from the lush meadows of the
rising ground.

It was a well-kept and lovely situation in which to
live and work, but Mr. T was not thinking of its per-
fections as he reached the barn that morning. Even the
pretty sight of a colt rolling from side to side in the
sandy paddock on his right only suggested fleetingly
to him that the poor critter likely had the stable-itch.

For in his hand was a piece of bad news for Julie Jefferson; and he was fonder of Julie—he had no family of his own—than he could have imagined possible before these past weeks had settled her into his life. Julie was the only girl he'd ever met whom he considered top-notch daughter material. The typed message he held concerned her real father . . . who must be quite a fellow, thought Mr. T, entering the barn, to own a daughter of such caliber.

She was saddling Curious Cottabus, a big brown gelding. "Morning, Mr. T," she said brightly, smiling at him across the horse.

"Morning, Julie. Can I see you for a minute in the remedy room?"

"Sure." She came out of the stall and walked down the wide aisle beside him to the cubbyhole where the medicines were kept. He shut the door behind them.

"Sit down, honey," he said, pushing an upturned bucket toward her with his foot. "I'm afraid I have some news for you that isn't so good."

"What is it?" she asked, standing still and looking into his eyes. "Bonnie?"

"No, no. Here," he said miserably, thrusting the paper at her. "It's a telegram. They just phoned it in. Secretary typed it out for you. Sit down."

She didn't, but remained standing as she read through the thing once and then again. Rollin Tolkov reread it himself, in his memory, as he watched her face go pale under the tan in the harsh light of the big naked bulb overhead.

RAND HURT BACK IN FALL FROM LADDER TWO DAYS AGO. BEAU NURSING HIM. DOCTOR SAYS IMMEDIATE OPERATION NECESSARY. WILL EVERETT.

Julie said "Oh!" and looked up at him.

"Come up to the house and call home," said Mr. T gently. "No use worrying yourself sick on that much information."

"Yes. Yes, I will, thanks."

He opened the door and gave her his arm.

"Monty's father doesn't waste words, does he?" said Mr. T bitterly. "Just enough to worry a person."

"He's a good man, really. It's just that—well, he

talks just like this telegram. Expects you to read between the words."

"Who is Beau?"

"Stash's oldest boy. He's been working as an apprentice jockey down here in Kentucky somewhere. I haven't seen him for ages. He must have just gone home. He's a g-good guy. Stash says he knows more than his old man about horses already." Julie was crying, but without tears. "Nobody knows more about horses than Stash, though."

"Use the phone in here," said her employer, opening the door to his private office. "I'll be right here, Julie."

"Thank you," she said, and went in. Not thinking too clearly, she dialed what she thought was Will Everett's number, but it was the phone in the St. Clair stable, and Stash answered. "That you, Julie? How are you?"

"Oh, Stash, I'm so *worried* about Dad! I just got this wire and it doesn't say anything!"

"Well, easy now, I'll tell you. It ain't so awful bad as it might have been, Julie," said Stash in his normal, easy tones. She was a little comforted at once. Stash always gave you the true impression about anything; he didn't make light of bad situations. "Your dad's restin' comfortable. But first thing of all, he got to take him a little operation, which the doc says is kind of a minor major one, you see? Else if he don't take it, he's not liable to walk much any more."

"Stash!" she yelped, horrified.

"But he *will* be all right, Julie, don't fret. He only needs this one little minor major piece o' surgical takin' care of. Meantime ol' Beau's doing for him better'n any nurse you could get. Beau treatin' him like he was as delicate and valuable as Tuxedo herself."

Julie giggled in spite of her fear. Tuxedo was the top stakes winner of the St. Clair string. "I know he would. Tell me about the accident, Stash, please."

"Well now, that was a plain piece of bad luck. He climbed up a ladder two days ago to put a big old punch bowl on the top shelf, forgettin' that that ladder was older than Methuselah. And it give way under him and he fell on his back. Kitty, she run for the doc, and he says Mr. Jefferson can rest at home, long as somebody's there to do for him, and needn't go in the hospital until it's time for that operation. He caught himself what they call a slippery disk."

"Slipped disk," Julie murmured to herself. She knew nothing about such a calamity, except the name: she was not at all sure what a disk was. "What do they do for that, Stash?" she asked.

"Well, they take it out, on account of it bein' too slippery, I s'pose, to do its job any more. Then they kind of fuse the two vertebras together so there won't be a gap in the old backbone. Then they sew him up and it's all done. Doc says he's not fussed up about it, that your dad's healthy as a well-bred shoat and twice as ornery, and with Beau keepin' him in bed he'll do fine, so long as he don't wait too long for the operation."

"How expensive is it, Stash?"

"Sounds to me like a whole heap of money," said Stash, concern creeping into his voice for the first time. "And I got to tell you, Julie, your dad's not easy in his mind about that part of it. I figure he isn't exactly the richest man in Ohio."

"He spent two hundred dollars on Bonnie and that was nearly all he had put away," Julie said. "I know the car isn't all paid for, and . . . Gosh, I don't know *how* much he has, Stash, but if he's worrying about money for the operation, then he mustn't have much. I'm going to pay him back for Bonnie as soon as she wins a race. But I guess two hundred, even, won't cover this?"

"Not near," said Stash. "He's talkin' about selling the antique emporium, and maybe his place over yonder, too."

"The shop and the house? Oh wow!" She stared at the phone. "Listen, Stash, don't let him even *think* of that! I'll get the money somehow." A brief terrible vision of herself selling Bonnie to Mr. T flitted through her mind. She shuddered. "Stash, should I come home?"

"No. Positively not. You been down there workin' such a short time, it'd fret Mr. Jefferson real bad to think he'd had a hand in makin' you quit, even for a couple days, Julie. He's proud as he can be of you bein' an assistant trainer at your age, and his mind got to be kept as easy as possible right now, don't it? Has that fine filly got herself squared away with the officials yet?"

"Yes. She's registered as Sunbonnet."

"Might think about racin' her, then."

"Oh, yes, I am. Any share of a purse would be enough to pay Dad's expenses. And he mustn't dream of selling the house, let alone the shop. You tell him, Stash, I'll get him the money. Tell him fierce and plain."

"Trust me."

"And I'll keep in touch with you, Stash. I guess I shouldn't call him."

"That's right, he can't get to a phone 'cept he has to, and it'd pain him bad to do it. He'll know you're thinkin' good thoughts about him, I'll see to that. And, Julie—don't lie awake in a stew over this, 'cause he's a tough bird and they ain't even dug the iron to make the pot to cook him in."

"Thank you, Stash. For everything. I'll go talk to Monty about a race for Bonnie. Bye." She hung up and sat there thinking hard. Finally she went out to tell Mr. T everything she knew.

"I can advance you the money, Julie," he said at once.

"No, that wouldn't be right. I have to get it myself."

"But—"

"It just wouldn't be right. I owe you so much already. After all, practically anyone else in your position would just have paid me two hundred dollars and taken Bonnie away from me. And you gave me, a girl-type kid, a responsible job, just on Monty's word that I was good with horses. No, I wouldn't ever feel good about it, Mr. T, even after I'd paid you back. I have to get the money myself. I owe so much to Dad, too, you see."

"You're quite a hardheaded little person," he said, chuckling. "If you were as intrigued by finance as you are by horses, I'd make you a partner in my firm today, and Uni-Tea would soon be bigger than Bell Telephone. All right, but come to me if you have too much trouble."

Julie emerged into the crisp autumn sunlight and padded briskly down to the big training track where

Monty was supervising the exercise boys who were working three horses into condition. He rounded the far turn and saw her waving to him. He let his mount, an exuberant little chestnut called Bandicoot, into a run.

"What's up? You look shaky," he said, arriving.

She told him quickly what she had heard. His face fell. Monty had been riding the clouds for three days, ever since he'd won his first race as trainer for Deepwater Farm, and so this news was doubly shocking.

"Can we enter Bonnie in a race? Real soon?"

"Let me think. Hey! There's a maiden race at Kandahar Park day after tomorrow," he told her. "For two-year-old fillies. Made to order."

"She'll have to be okayed out of the starting gate before then."

"She'll make it. Wait a minute . . . is it a claiming race?" He scowled thoughtfully. "No, it isn't. That's all right, then. Why don't you go call Jack Lillie right away? You know him, the Racing Secretary at Kandahar."

"Boy, do I know him. He was there that fateful night," said Julie, referring to the evening when they'd trapped the crooked Homer and Matthews into trying to steal Bonnie. "I'll call him."

And fifteen minutes later she was whispering into Bonnie's ear the joyous news that she would soon be running in her first real, genuine, professional race. And, of course, winning it.

Any other possibility Julie resolutely refused to consider.

Chapter II

Number 677820, Sunbonnet herself, walked sedately out of the chute and down the track toward the starting gate at Kandahar Park. Rider, Montgomery Everett, licensed trainer, Deepwater Farm. Owner, now leaning on the rail and holding her breath, Julie Jefferson, likewise of Deepwater Farm, full of pride and fearfulness.

Months ago Bonnie had been given her first lessons in the mysteries of the gate. Day after day she had been walked in and out of one of the narrow stalls of the gate at St. Clair Farm. She had stood in its confines, with the door open before her, and eaten numerous carrots from Julie's hand, first nervously, then with vast confidence. There came a day when, released onto the track, she had trotted over to the gate and gone in herself, whinnying eagerly. That day she'd gotten three carrots and two lumps of sugar.

The next afternoon she was ridden into it, being patted all the way, to discover that the door was closed in front of her. The ears had gone back nervously, momentarily; then a carrot had appeared under her nose, and all was well. Her friend Stash had manually opened and closed the door as she stood there munching. Undisturbed, she demanded another treat.

Then a frightening thing had occurred. Stash had closed the door *behind* her too. She was a poor lorn horse in a steel box.

Bonnie objected loudly, shifted back and forth, stamped, and did everything she could think of to register her sharp criticism of the whole business except rearing. (She had only once reared under Julie, the day she had first seen a raccoon—a terrifying sight indeed to a civilized filly. Julie had forgiven her on the spot.) Nothing happened. At last Stash opened the door before her, and she jumped out, shaking her head reproachfully.

This experience was repeated until she was quite used to being shut into the thing. Then Stash had gone to the electrical controls and let the doors fly open several times, whereat Julie had urged her to leap forward into the free sunshine. This, too, Bonnie had grown accustomed to.

Then the last weird part of the whole rigmarole was laid on her. As the doors swept out, a bell rang. Bonnie, startled, burst into a run. This had evidently pleased the girl in the saddle, so Bonnie had done it again. And again. And again. With many carrots for reward.

Thus Bonnie had learned to break cleanly· and fast from the great metal barrier where she would begin each race of her career. A couple of times since she had moved to Deepwater she had practiced it all over again, patiently proving that her memory was perfectly good. Now she had to prove it to the starter of Kandahar Park.

Monty picked her up to a trot. She came to the gate and almost automatically went into one of the stalls. The door closed behind her. She waited serenely, the model of a well-behaved horse, an old-timer at the business. The bell rang, the door whipped open, and Bonnie roared out and down the track like a beautiful rocket.

Julie looked up at the starter on his tower. "How was she?"

He grinned down. "Does she do that every time? No fuss?"

"Yes, sir."

"I'm happy. She's okayed."

"Whew," said Julie fervently. Her father's operation was assured. The maiden race was next day.

But in the morning her friend Max McGraw, the boss

of the stable area, sought her out with bad news. She was grooming Bonnie in the stall when he found her. "Julie, I've just heard. There are enough entrants to fill the race without your filly. She can't run."

"But she has to run! She just *has* to!" Julie exclaimed.

"Tough luck, but she can't. Her name was at the bottom of the list, because she was entered so late." He gave her a rueful grimace. "That's the breaks. The racing cookie often crumbles in your hands, Julie. Have to roll with the bad times."

"Yes. You sure do. Gosh, what'll I do?" She told him briefly why she needed money.

He frowned at Bonnie for a minute. Then he said, "Come along to the office, we'll look at the condition book." This is the book, published by the track, that lists the conditions of the races for a meeting. "We'll study it hard, but . . . well, I don't know," he said dubiously, as they walked side by side down the broad aisle toward his headquarters. Horses nickered over their stall doors as they passed, begging for tidbits, but Julie was too crushed to notice. They sat down and pored over the condition book.

"I don't see anything suitable at all," Max said at last. "Unless—"

"I'll try anything," she prompted him.

"This twenty-thousand-dollar claiming race tomorrow. It's a real gamble, but if you need money fast, it's the only answer."

Julie stared at the print before her, thinking hard. Any horse entered in a claiming race can be bought for the amount at which it is entered—in the case of this race, a top-and-bottom one, each horse was valued at $20,000, one twentieth of Bonnie's original yearling price. Anyone wishing to buy her could put up that sum, together with his claim, before the race, and lead her away at the finish.

"It's a gamble," Max repeated, "and I'm not recommending it, you understand. I'm only saying it's the only race she could possibly run in during this meeting. I'd certainly hate to see you lose her, Julie, after all you've been through with her."

"How big a gamble is it? Let's figure it out," Julie

said. "Who knows who Sunbonnet really is? The Jockey Club——"

"Happily, they have the closest mouths in the business."

"And you."

The large brown man laughed. "I just *sound* like a gossipy old windbag. I haven't told the tale to a soul."

"Then there's Mr. T and Monty and Stash, and Leon and Beau and a few more of the gang back home at St. Clair. They're all right. And of course there's Zeke and Alex Homer, but they're in jail."

"It's too many people, Julie, to say for certain that no one else has heard your Bonnie's the Bold Ruler filly that cost Tolkov the record price at Saratoga. We can chew it around as much as we like, but the fact is going to remain, it's a gamble."

"Nobody would claim her for that amount if he didn't know about her true identity, would they?"

"Not a chance."

"Then . . . then I'll enter her in the claiming race," said Julie firmly. She thought of Rand Jefferson suffering quietly with a fire of pain in his back. Any chance was worth taking. Even with Bonnie. "Can you direct me to whoever might manage to get her into it this late?"

"Go over to Jack Lillie's office and see if you can still fill out an entry blank. There's certainly room in that race for a good dark horse; there wasn't an overabundance of twenty-thousand-dollar horses this time." Max tugged at his ear thoughtfully. "You might trust Jack with the whole story. Ever since Star Princess doubled for Bonnie to nail a pair of unsavory characters here that wild night, Jack has been wistfully waiting to hear what it was all about. Get his opinion on risking her in a claimer, too."

"I'm certainly grateful to you for all your help, Mr. McGraw."

"Wait till you've got a pocketful of bills," he said, "and your filly safe home in her stall; then thank me."

She walked the long distance around the far turn and the nursery course, skirted the jammed, thunderous grandstand, and went into the big complex of buildings housing the offices, cafeteria, pari-mutuel machines, press room, and clubhouse. Jack Lillie was not in his office. She sat down to fill out an entry form for Sunbonnet.

At noon the Racing Secretary appeared, a corned beef sandwich in hand and an expression of mild harassment on his face. "Hi, Miss Jefferson. Want to see me? Mind if I eat? Glory, what a day! Too bad about your filly being cancelled. Happens. Miss Ward, get Rowland on the phone. Wow, starved! Come in, Miss Jefferson." He went into his tiny private office, closed the door behind them. "Understand you work for Tolkov now. Good show. Think he'd let you tell me what it was that happened on my track that night, when Zeke Matthews got himself shot all over my shed row?"

Between his telephone calls, she told him the story of Star Princess. They discussed Bonnie's participation in the claiming race. Lillie was of the opinion that Sunbonnet, owner J. Jefferson, would not attract $20,000 of anybody's money. "Unless someone is in the know, and watching for a chance like this," he said. "Which dosen't seem likely to me. However, I'll go along with McGraw: it's a gamble, and only you can make the decision. Far as the race goes, I can put you into it. We have a slim field in that one."

"Fine. I'll do it. I have to."

"You're in, then. Sorry, I have to run. Good luck, Miss Jefferson." And he was gone, skimming through a sheaf of papers as he walked down the corridor.

Julie returned to the stable area and met Monty, who had just arrived with three of Mr. T's racers, Sugar Candy, Dunt Esk, and Julie's favorite, Curious Cottabus. They were racing tomorrow and the next day. She got them two orange sodas and brought Monty up to date.

The claiming race worried him mildly, but her earnestness about paying for Rand's operation could not be argued with. She was desperate enough to fidget, a bad sign in Julie; the only other time he'd seen her drum her fingers on her blue-jeaned knee, she'd thought that Bonnie was in deadly danger. Monty said as heartily as he could, "She'll win, I know she will. Isn't she

Starcrossed's daughter? And nobody's going to claim a maiden, who not only hasn't won, but hasn't even *raced* before, for twenty grand. Why, if Jack Lillie hadn't known her actual breeding, he wouldn't even have let her in a claiming race for that high a figure!"

"So people will guess that she's from very good stock. Maybe I shouldn't have done it," said the girl soberly, "it's such a terrible chance to take. But I have to, don't I? Right? Right."

Monty, afraid he's babble on till he said something that would really spook her, wisely shut up, and they began to fuss together over Bonnie and the Deepwater horses.

Bonnie's race was the third on the program, scheduled to start at two thirty. It was a balmy day for so late in the year, and the stands were aflash with gaudy, summery colors. At two fifteen, a tall, loose-limbed man with a western suntan and a broadbrimmed hat to match, whose blue eyes were so washed out in the dark brown of his lean face that they appeared almost white, walked through the paddock, glancing at the horses being saddled.

No one challenged his presence there. He was a trainer named Rodinbaugh who was well known at the track. When he stopped and stared for thirty full seconds at Bonnie, nobody even noticed.

Leaving the paddock, moving now at a powerful lope that opened the crowds before him, he made for the administration offices. Here he snatched a claim sheet from the table, filled it out hurriedly, and strode to the time clock. There was another man there before him, and he was forced to wait. Two twenty-five was the deadline for claims. The clock said two twenty-three. As Rodinbaugh watched, the minute jerked forward. *One minute left.*

"Will you move your crawling, miserable, worthless carcass?" he growled into the ear of the oblivious gentleman ahead of him, who jumped and whirled round. "What the blazes are you doing, learning how to tell time?" Rodinbaugh demanded. His voice was low and coarse in texture, as though his throat were lined with tweed, rather dirty tweed too. "Come on!"

"There's something wrong with the clock," said the other, nervously pushing his claim in again. There was the mechanical sound that indicates a time clock doing its job calmly and efficiently. "Oh," said the man ahead of Rodinbaugh, staring at it. "Well. It wasn't working before." Then he moved off, as a snarl from the tall pale-eyed man indicated that he might well be booted out of the way.

Rodinbaugh jammed his paper into the narrow maw of the machine. Nothing happened. He poked it impatiently in and out, in and out. He took it out and straightened its edges carefully and inserted it again. No sound from the clock. Then the hand jumped forward.

Two twenty-five. Deadline.

Rodinbaugh said something picturesque under his breath. The mechanism was not going to work again. And without a time stamp, no claim is valid. Rodinbaugh glared at the clock as though he meant to stick his fist through its stupid face, and rammed the paper in and out until it began to crumple. Then the Claims Secretary appeared from another office.

"Something wrong?"

"I've been trying to get this stamped, but your clock's gone bad on you. I was in plenty of time—"

"Sorry, I'm sure you were; it's only a few seconds after two twenty-five now, and I did hear you at it before. Let me have that." Rodinbaugh handed him the claim sheet. The secretary wrote the time, initialed it, and deposited the paper in the claim box.

Rodinbaugh exhaled with relief. "Thanks. If you hadn't been here, I'd have been in trouble."

"I'll get a man on that clock right away. Good luck," said the secretary genially, disappearing once more.

Rodinbaugh left the offices with a peculiar smile on his thin face. No one could have called it a pleasant smile, except, perhaps, a lenient crocodile.

Chapter III

The horses had moved onto the track and were loosening up in their progress toward the starting gate. Many of them followed lead ponies; Bonnie was one of these, for they did not know how she would react to her first appearance before a vast crowd of noisy people. Although a little startled by them, Bonnie nevertheless remained a lady, jigging up to her cubicle in the gate most demurely. By post time they were nearly ready to start.

Bonnie's jockey was Irv Blaise, who had come down with Monty to ride the Cottabus. He was a veteran, at 98 pounds tiny even among jockeys, with good hands, good nerves, and plenty of horse sense. He had made himself acquainted with Bonnie two weeks before, although he had not ridden her until today.

Monty and Julie watched as the horses got off to a good start. The field was so bunched that it was all but impossible to tell what horse was running where. Monty was concerned that Bonnie might not perform well in her first outing against an experienced field; he hoped that they weren't asking too much of her. Julie had vast faith in her filly's ability and fighting heart; she was nervous, yes, but excitement accounted for most of that.

They stayed bunched for longer than ordinary. Then one and soon another dropped behind, but the pack held close; a thick clot of them swept around the clubhouse turn and into the backstretch. Bonnie, his field glasses told Monty, was in a blind switch, boxed in on all sides, and could not get clear to run. There was a great deal of bumping due to the close quarters. He was afraid that not only would she not have the chance to be out in the open, but that all the banging and jostling would make her frightened of running tightly with other horses.

"Come on, open up, open up," he was yelling, without knowing that a sound was coming out of him. "Let 'er loose!"

"Where *is* she?" Julie demanded.

"What?" he said, startled, as she hit him in the ribs.

"Where's Bonnie?"

"Right smack in the middle of all that." He had lost her with the glasses. Now he picked her up again. They had gone the entire length of the backstretch in a close, companionable gang; at last at the start of the far turn they opened up a bit. The gray to Bonnie's right began to tire and dropped back, leaving a hole that offered escape. It would be the long way round, skirting the gang, but it was the only way. Irv took her right and curved her along the outside rail, and she stretched out in that grand long powerful stride till she was passing them, now coming down the home-stretch and passing, coming on like the wind, and Julie joggled him so wildly that Monty lost the field completely and dropped the glasses on his chest because he didn't need them now anyway, and she kept coming and there was no doubt that she would place at least; then the leader put on a blaze of speed and drew away from the pack behind him, and Bonnie near the outside rail drove forward as though she had just found her gait, and the two of them left the others nowhere.

Julie screamed encouragement into the crashing thunder of the crowd.

Bonnie gained and gained and the two of them passed the tote board neck and neck, and at the finish she was in the lead by a good half-length, and the noise was really stunning.

"She won!" Julie hugged Monty with glee. "She actually *won!*"

"She sure did."

"I can't believe it. But she did."

"She is plain out of sight," said Monty, breathless.

"She's going to be the champion. She's going to take the Triple Crown when she's three!"

"One race at a time," said Monty. "Let's get down to the winner's circle and congratulate Irv."

"And Bonnie." They took hands and hurried down through the crowd. Julie posed for the traditional photograph with her filly, trying not to look *too* smug.

Irv was saying over and over, "I never sat on such a sweet little lightning flash before, not in all my days. She is A-OK." He was not addressing anyone in particular, unless it was Bonnie herself. Julie kissed Bonnie on the nose and Monty pumped Irv's hand fiercely.

Then Irv dismounted and they all talked at once, and a groom came through the concentration of people around them with a halter in his hand; and he slipped it on Bonnie and led her away.

He had not looked at any of them, and they, dumbfounded, had not spoken to him. It was like a fragment of nightmare suddenly slid into the center of this sunny, wonderful day. Nobody moved for a moment, until Julie gave a preliminary gasp and said shrilly, "Who was that?"

Monty was unable to make a sound. Irv said in a flat voice, "Looks like she's been claimed, Julie."

"But who—who could have known—who would have done—"

"We'll find out," said Monty, suddenly becoming grim and competent. "Something's fishy about this."

"She's gone," wailed Julie, "she's gone! My Bonnie's gone!" With a sob, she plunged blindly into the throng and vanished, in the wake of the filly.

Monty, after a word to Irv Blaise, followed her, but the spectators were so thick that he could not see her bright blond head anywhere. He had a hunch that she'd head for Bonnie's stall, however, unless she spotted the groom and assaulted him; so he made for the barn and ten minutes later discovered Julie sitting on Bonnie's straw crying bitterly.

"Cut it out, Julie," he said, patting her shoulder, "she isn't lost yet. We'll—"

"Yes she is. Anyone with twenty thousand dollars could have claimed her, any owner or authorized agent, and you know it. I knew it when I entered her. B-but I had to get the money for Dad. And s-so she's gone."

"I tell you, there's something rotten somewhere, and I'm going to find out what. Nobody who knew about her breeding legitimately would have claimed her. It has to be somebody connected with Homer or Matthews, Julie, and if they are, they're crooked as a snake with colic. You stay here and mind the Deepwater horses while I go dig into things."

"All right," said Julie, sniffling, "but it's no use. I know it. Bonnie's gone." She stared up at him. Slowly her face untwisted itself from the sorrow. "I'm sorry, Monty. Stash would be ashamed of me, thinking bad thoughts like that. Go ahead and check on it. I'm all right."

"Good girl." First he went down the double row of stalls to make certain Bonnie had not been stabled here. Then he went out to investigate the rest of the shed row. He found Bonnie being cooled out by the same groom, with a tall brown man watching her thoughtfully. On a hunch, he said to the man, "You the one who claimed her?"

Pale eyes flicked over him. "Who's asking?"

"Monty Everett, Deepwater Farm."

"And why do you care who claimed her?" the fellow asked in a low, rough voice.

"That's my business."

"If you're worried about the tack that was on her, that'll be returned. You can have it now." The light-colored eyes laughed at him, without humor. "Want more information? Come back with a cop."

"That's a queer thing to say," Monty told him. "All I asked was whether you claimed her. Do you have a guilty conscience, or what? Something shady about the claim, maybe?"

"Go get yourself an ice cream cone, sonny," said

Rodinbaugh, thumbing back the big brim of his hat and grinning. "Take your saddle with you, if you can lift it."

Monty, baffled and more suspicious than before, picked up the bridle and saddle, which weighed about two pounds, and walked back to the empty stall where Julie waited. He told Julie that he had located Bonnie, who was looking fine, and a stranger who refused to answer questions. "So there's hope," he said, "because if he's entirely aboveboard, why the secrecy? I'm going to see Jack Lillie." He left her a little more cheerful than she had been before.

Monty went directly to the office of Kandahar Park's Racing Secretary. Here he told Jack Lillie, who was somewhat less harried than usual, how he had sought out Bonnie's claimer, who had been evasive and insulting. Lillie asked for a description. "Yes," he said, "that's what's-his-name, Rodinbaugh. Works for Jonas Black. An unpleasant kind of fellow, always looks as though his trigger finger itches. It's highly irregular, but let's look over the claim sheet." While they waited for this to be brought, Lillie asked for various details of Bonnie's history.

"I believe I have the whole picture now," he said, as a girl brought in the claim sheets for that day. "Your hunch may be right, Everett, because twenty thousand is ridiculous for an unknown horse—though by this time, after that great finish, she's hardly unknown any more—but Black's reputation is perfectly all right, and this man Rodinbaugh is only curt and tough-looking; he has no record of anything remotely criminal, obviously, or he wouldn't be here at the track." He shuffled the papers. "Here it is. No stamp? Wait a minute."

He got on the phone to a member of his staff. After listening a minute, he rang off. "It's kosher enough. The clock wasn't working and the Claims Secretary okayed it by hand, but he says Rodinbaugh was in plenty of time. Nothing there."

"Is there anything I can do?" asked Monty.

"Not officially. We have nothing to go on but the

horse's very rough time with those two crooked cus-
tomers who stole her. However," he said, drooping
one eyelid, "if you, as a private citizen, want to give
Jonas Black a call, and ask him some penetrating
questions, entirely on your own and without the urging
of any official of Kandahar, nobody could possibly
stop you. It would be easy enough to find out his
phone number." Lillie took a book from his desk and
flipped the pages. "For instance, if you looked on line
four here, and made a note of those ten numerals, it
would hardly be illegal, would it? Certainly not. It
would simply save you calling an operator for the
number." He picked up his telephone and asked for
a line; then he handed it to Monty, who could hear
the dial tone humming quietly. "You're quite at liberty
to use this if you have any personal calls to make
that are aimed at the good of the track," he said,
getting up, "and I shall be gone for ten minutes. I do
not urge you to do anything at all, except whatever
it is you intend to do, and I have nothing to do with
that. Unless you discover something that smells funny."

He walked toward the door of his office. Monty
said, "Sir?"

"Yes?"

"I don't understand why you're doing this exactly."

"I'm not doing anything. *You* are. And I happen to
think that Miss Jefferson has had quite enough hard
luck this year, for such a beguiling and obviously
honest child. And I don't like men who think they're
the incarnation of some nineteenth-century gunman out
of the Old West. And I do like clean, straightforward,
untarnished racing, and great horses, and young people
who work for both. And finally, I'm not doing anything
except go out for a Coke, and I have no control over
you whatever." He closed the door behind him.

Monty dialed the area code and the number. A
woman said, "Jonas Black's office."

"May I speak to Mr. Black? This is Montgomery
Everett, calling from Kandahar Park in Kentucky."

"I'm sorry, Mr. Black has been out of town on
business for six weeks."

"Can you tell me where he can be reached?"

"I'm sorry, I am not authorized to give out that information."

"When will he be back, then?"

"I'm sorry, I am not authorized to give out that information, either."

"Well, would *anyone* be able to tell me?" said Monty desperately.

"I'm sorry, I am not authorized—"

"To give out that information, either," said Monty. "Many thanks, ma'am." He hung up.

When Jack Lillie returned, Monty was pacing. The office was only three long paces wide, but Monty was managing to imitate a caged lion. "Black's out of town. They wouldn't say where, or for how long." He halted, to glare at the Racing Secretary. "I *know* that somebody's up to no good!" he exclaimed.

"Well, officially and unofficially I can assure you it isn't Jonas Black." Lillie sat down at his desk, checked the book he had searched before, and wrote something down on a piece of paper. "He's often clear out of the country, and he may be now. If so, I doubt very strongly that he authorized the purchase of Sunbonnet. If he didn't, the claim is invalid; Rodinbaugh can't claim her himself, especially not if he uses Black's name without authority. Why, he could lose his trainer's license for good if he pulled such a stunt."

"We don't know that he did."

"No, it's all suspicion, and it mustn't go any further than that door, Everett, not yet anyway. What happens now is up to you. I have nothing to do with it. If I hand you the home telephone number of Jonas Black, for example, and mention that his wife doesn't usually travel with him because she stays home to look after the kids," said Lillie, doing so, "it's only to save you all the fuss of arguing with some New York operator. It isn't to be taken from this that I agree with your unfounded suspicion that there is a long tall fly buzzing in the ointment. If that's the figure of speech I'm looking for. Well! Keep me informed. Unofficially. And I'll drag my heels just a little on this claim." He shook hands with Monty. "Best of luck, Everett. And try to keep Miss Jefferson from glooming too deeply. Maybe things will work out when you track down old Jonas."

"I hope so," said Monty, and with hearty thanks for all the help, he left Lillie's office.

Julie listened to his story, and said, "Monty, suppose that Rodinbaugh is in league with Homer or Matthews, and they're directing him from prison, and he got his hands on Bonnie so that he can shoot her and—"

"Julie! Cool it. You're still living back there when Star Princess and Bonnie had been exchanged and— my gosh! Where would the profit be in that, for anybody, let alone two guys in jail?"

"Revenge," said Julie darkly.

"You are just scaring yourself for no reason at all," Monty snapped at her. "Look: the *only* bit of reason we have for thinking there's dirty work is that Jonas Black is out of town. But Lillie could be entirely wrong about it, and Rodinbaugh may have had a telegram or a phone call to buy Bonnie. Except for that, the whole business is just another horse claimed because—well, because she looks good, or because somebody heard about her breeding. We don't know that that didn't happen, after all; a lot of people know about it by now."

"The whole thing is just reeking of crime and mischief," Julie said with finality. "Look at how Rodinbaugh acted with you when all you asked was who'd bought her."

"That's his way. Plenty of people are nasty without being crooked."

"You don't believe for a minute that the claim was only an ordinary claim."

Monty scowled at her so hard that his face hurt. At last he said, "Of course I don't."

"Then what do we do?"

"I call Mrs. Black."

"No," Julie said, "*I* call her." She put her hand on his arm. "Thanks, Monty, anyway. But Bonnie is— was—*is* my horse."

"But—"

"You have work to do for Mr. T here. You can't go around forever getting me and my horse out of jams. I'll call Mrs. Black and take it from there." She smiled, a little shakily, at him. "I've had my cry, Monty. I'm all right now. I can handle it."

He drew a deep breath. "Yes," he said, "I guess you can, Julie Jefferson. I guess you can."

Chapter IV

Julie was informed officially that her share of the purse for the race that Bonnie had won would be $5,000. Even in the middle of all her fresh and terrible trouble, she was thunderstruck by that. Five thousand dollars! Rand Jefferson's operation was assured, his home and store saved, and . . . and . . . well, it seemed to her that such an enormous sum of money would last for years and years.

She went through all the formalities that were necessary at that point, and when at last she had some free time, put in a call to Mrs. Jonas Black at the number furnished by the Racing Secretary. Mrs. Black seemed pleasant. "Yes, my dear, I've heard of Deepwater Farm. Rollin Tolkov owns it, doesn't he? I don't pay a great deal of attention to my husband's affairs, I admit, but I do know that. Rollin is an old friend."

Julie wondered briefly if the news had come to Mr. Black from Mr. T; but that was unlikely. Or was it? If they were good friends . . . He might have told them the story of Bonnie's adventures, just in conversation, and there certainly wouldn't have been any obligation to pass the word back to Julie that he'd done so. But if they were good friends, would Mr. Black have told his trainer to watch for a chance to get hold of Bonnie? It hardly seemed possible.

But of course it *was* possible. Mr. T wouldn't have told them in confidence. The whole story wasn't a *secret*, after all. Julie realized that she had entered Bonnie in the claiming race with the idea that her bloodlines were a mystery to all but a handful of people. That wasn't necessarily true! She simply had assumed that Mr. T had told no one. But maybe he had. Why shouldn't he, after such a series of hair-raising experiences, tell the story to his friends?

If he had, and if Mr. Black had determined to get hold of Bonnie, there was nothing that Jack Lillie or Monty or she or Mr. T himself could ever do about it now.

"What?" she said abruptly into the phone, as she became conscious of the voice raised on the other end of the line.

"I said, what did you want to ask my husband?" it said sharply.

"I'm sorry, my mind wandered for a minute. Well, his trainer claimed my horse, and I wanted to talk to Mr. Black about it."

"Who, Rodinbaugh? He claims your horse did what?"

"No, no, he claimed her. In a race."

"I'm afraid I don't understand racing slang, my dear," said the voice in a helpless, friendly way. "But Jo ought to be home tonight. He's been up in Canada, you know, buying horses left and right, I suppose. He gets carried away, he loves them so."

Oh, my! thought Julie, maybe he was carried away when Mr. T told him about the $400,000 filly.

"When could I call him?"

"I don't know for sure. He said tonight. At least I *think* it was tonight. What day is this? Yes, he definitely said tonight. Is it very important, what you want to ask him?"

"Oh, yes."

"Perhaps you'd better come into town, then. Jo doesn't care for telephones. For a man of fifty (oh dear, I'm always giving his age away!) he can be the most old-fashioned person. . . . Yes, that's it, you come into town and speak with him. What was your name again, dear?"

"Julie Jefferson."

"Mrs. Jefferson?"

"Miss." Julie could not help giggling. "I'm seventeen."

"Oh!" said the voice, which had been growing slightly frosty. "Splendid! Then you just come in this evening, and we'll see what Jo can tell you about your horse, shall we? Fine! Good-bye," said Mrs. Black brightly, and rung off.

"Oh wow," said Julie, hanging up slowly. She couldn't go all the way to New York just to ask—

On the other hand, she thought, staring at the phone and thinking hard, she *could*. Bonnie had won $5,000 for her today. And if she met Mr. Black, caught him off guard and asked him two or three fast, penetrating questions about Rodinbaugh and Bonnie, she might learn far more than she would talking long-distance to someone who didn't like telephones.

The longer she worried it around in her mind, the sounder the idea seemed. The air field was only a few miles away. She checked with them about schedules and fares. She tossed a toothbrush and an extra dress into Monty's briefcase, left a message for him with the Deepwater groom who was working on Sugar Candy (who had placed in the race he'd been in, the one after Bonnie's), and drove out to the airport.

All the way to New York she framed and reframed the questions she would ask. It was so important, and the loss of Bonnie so overwhelming, that Julie scarcely noticed the details of her first trip in an airplane. Only as the jet touched down at Kennedy did it occur to her that she had just been farther off the ground than she had ever been before.

"Well," she told herself in consolation, "I'll notice things on the way back to Kentucky." If, of course, anything good came of this journey.

A taxi deposited her in front of a gigantic apartment building on Sutton Place. Shortly she found herself in a sixty-foot living room overlooking the East River, with a tawny short-haired cat regarding her superciliously and two girls in their early teens treating her like one of the family. Mrs. Black herself was fortyish, plump and jolly and a little scatterbrained.

"Sit down, Miss Jefferson. Would you like some orange soda? Pink grapefruit, perhaps? May I call you Juliet?"

"Julie," said Julie.

"Do you really own a *horse*?" one of the girls asked her.

"I did—"

"A boy or a girl horse?" asked the other, breathless with awe.

"A filly. I—"

"Is that a boy or a girl?"

"A girl," said Julie, laughing in spite of herself.

"What color?"

"Bay."

"But what color's *that*?"

"She's a beautiful reddish brown, with mahogany glints in her coat, and she's tall, over sixteen hands."

One of the girls looked at her own long-fingered hand and frowned. "Seven inches times sixteen is—" The other one said, "A hand is four inches, silly."

"Mine isn't."

"Well, hold it sideways."

"Oh. How old is your horse?"

"Here, Juliet," said Mrs. Black, holding out a glass of pink soft drink. "Or would you like a candy bar? In addition to, or instead of?"

In an hour, Julie had grown used to being addressed as "Juliet," and had become adept at answering questions in six words or less, all she usually had time for. But she had completely forgotten the crossexamination she had worked out for use on Mr. Black, so that when he arrived at last, and stood just inside the door being engulfed by children, wife, and cat, Julie stared blankly at a huge abstract-art painting that was evidently an emerald goldfish with the bends. She realized that everything had gone out of her head except the fast query-and-answer game she'd been playing with the three Black females. And it was impossible to concentrate in the din of the homecoming.

Well, they did seem like a nice family, and maybe just a couple of straightforward questions about Rodinbaugh and Bonnie would be enough. Julie reminded herself that she wasn't engaged in dueling with crooks any longer, as far as she knew. And Jack Lillie had vouched for Jonas Black.

The turmoil of people and cat moved slowly into the vast living room. "Jo, I want you to meet our dear friend, Juliet Jefferson," said Mrs. Black.

"Julie," said Julie a final time, smiling shakily at him as they shook hands. This was it. The truth was here at last, waiting to be unveiled.

"Nice to meet you," said Jonas Black warmly. He was a square, gray-haired man with a face that had been whipped to a permanent scarlet by plenty of outdoor years. Julie liked him at once. "Staying to dinner?" he asked her, as though it were a mere formality because she certainly *must* stay. "Good," he said, nodding heartily, although she hadn't said yes or no, "that's settled. There is roast beef, isn't there?" he went on, addressing his wife. "I'm famished." Then he vanished, carrying his big suitcase as easily as if it had been the tawny cat.

"How do you like your roast beef?" Mrs. Black asked. "Medium rare all right? Splendid!"

"Do you jump?" asked one of the girls. "My friend Cecily jumps. I wish I could jump."

"I haven't learned yet," said Julie, correctly interpreting this as a return to the horse topic. "My horse is a racer."

"Sprinter or router?" asked the older girl, who had a smattering of horse terms at her command and plainly felt smug about them. Julie was mildly astonished at their broad ignorance of horses. Their father, after all, was a fairly wealthy owner, and they must have been surrounded from birth with an atmosphere of horse.

At dinner she found out from the general conversation that until quite recently the girls had resisted everything equine. Evidently it had been a case of Daddy's business affairs being of no earthly interest to his daughters (Julie recollected a friend of hers who had failed geometry twice running, thus disappointing her father horribly—he was a geometry teacher). But then the younger girl's pal Cecily had acquired a jumper, and suddenly horses were terribly important.

Julie was placed between them, at their firm demand, and through the soup and salad courses was bombarded with fresh requests for information. Jonas Black observed her from the head of the table with a slowly broadening smile as she, a little flustered, rattled off the responses. At last, as the roast beef was being sliced, he cleared his throat loudly and said, "They have now asked you twenty times as many questions about horses as they've asked me in a lifetime. I think you'd better take a long breath and the fifth amendment. Don't tell 'em another thing till dessert."

"Daddy!" both girls exclaimed angrily.

"She knows *all* about horses," one added.

"I think she does, indeed," said Jonas. "Are you connected with racing, or is your family, Julie?"

"I work for Rollin Tolkov."

"You do? You're a lucky girl," he said. Did a shadow of suspicion, or fright, perhaps, appear on his red face?

No. Julie admitted to herself that his expression was completely without guile. "I want to congratulate you, by the way," she said to him, "on your latest acquisition."

"Heard about her, eh? She's a beauty," said Jonas. He pitched into the meat, of which about three pounds had been laid before him. "Going to win me a lot of races, I'm sure of that. Great ancestry."

Julie lifted a forkful of meat and laid it down again. There was a dreadful hollow in her stomach, the kind that food wouldn't fill. "Yes, it is," she said, hearing her voice shake. He knew about Bonnie. There was nothing illegal or shady about Rodinbaugh's claim, then. "Wh-where did you hear about her?" she asked.

"That's a mild coincidence. Rollin told me about her; first, that is. The idea of owning her was exciting, I must say. A filly, after all, out of—"

"Is this meal to be eaten to the tune of nothing but horses, horses, horses?" Mrs. Black said to the table at large. "I have seldom felt myself so outnumbered!"

"Sorry, love," said Jonas, laughing.

"Tell us about your Canadian trip," said his wife. "Leaving out, if possible, the horses."

Julie ate a few bites, in order not to seem ungrateful for the food, which was probably delicious if she could have tasted it. Well, Bonnie was gone, then, really gone. All that Julie could ever do for her again was

pray that the nasty-seeming trainer, Rodinbaugh, would
be kind to her. She would have to find out about him
from Mr. Black, who was evidently a good man in
spite of his taking advantage of Mr. T's information to
do such a low trick as to claim Bonnie. . . .

She could not bring up the subject of horses again
at the table, for Mrs. Black was entranced with her
husband's Canadian stories. They had a fancy dessert
composed of ice cream and meringue and fruit and
various other goodies, most of which Julie slipped to
the younger Black girl when no one was looking. By
this time she was almost physically sick. The thought of
Bonnie living somewhere far away from her—of only
seeing her now and then at racetracks, if at all—of
never knowing how she was being treated, or whether
she was ever given her favorite treat, gumdrops—of not
being able to say Good night to her any more—it could
not be borne. Julie felt she would have to get away
soon and let herself cry long and hard, even if it was
in the waiting room of the airport.

"You're staying the night, of course," said Mrs.
Black to her as they walked down the little ramp
to the huge living room again.

"Oh, I'm sorry, but I can't. I have to catch a plane
at—"

"Nonsense," said Jonas Black heartily, "you have
to stay and tell me about Rollin. Bring me up to date.
How's his Cottabus doing these days?"

"The Cottabus is fine, thanks." She couldn't stay
here; she'd disgrace herself and never be able to explain why.

But maybe if she wept bitterly enough, he'd change
his mind and unclaim Bonnie, seeing how much she
loved the horse.

Stop trying to make a fairy tale out of it, she told
herself sharply. This is not only Real Life, it's Big Business. And Bonnie is going to be too productive a gold
mine for anyone to give her away for a few salt
tears.

She discovered that Mrs. Black had taken her air-
lines ticket and was already telephoning Kennedy to
change her flight from midnight to tomorrow morning

at eleven. She protested, without result. The hospitality was too powerful to buck.

Jonas took her arm and sat her down on the big gold sofa. "I know I'm going to be grateful to old Rollin for telling me about that filly," he said. "You tell him so, too. It was decent of him not to grab her for himself."

"I thought so," said Julie dismally.

"You see, her story wasn't known to many people until this week. Nobody had paid much attention to her."

"Except me," said Julie, all but inaudibly.

"You too? Say, then, you'll have to let me put a bet or two on her for you, as an old friend!"

"A very old friend," said Julie, "and getting older by the minute."

He laughed politely, as though he didn't quite understand her. "It isn't every day that one of Greeting Card's fillies goes unidentified until she's three, and then is authenticated with so little fanfare, I can tell you."

"Greeting Card?" she repeated vaguely.

"Why, yes. My filly's one of his get, didn't you know that?"

She stared at him, feeling her face go pale. "What filly?" she demanded.

"I Presume." He looked at her curiously for a few seconds and then added, "Out of the great mare Dr. Livingstone, you know."

"She's English," said Julie automatically, while her brains went into a whirl of unbelief. "I think we've been talking about two different fillies, sir."

"I only bought the one, the whole time I was in Canada—a three-year-old named I Presume, by Greeting Card out of Dr. Livingstone."

"Then you haven't bought Sunbonnet? Didn't Mr. T tell you about her?"

"Sunbonnet?" It was his turn to repeat a name blankly.

"Yes, the Bold Ruler filly. Rodinbaugh claimed her for you today."

"*What?*" The square red-faced man cocked his head at her as if she had begun speaking pig Latin.

"Yes. That's why I came here, to find out about it. He claimed my horse Sunbonnet, who shouldn't have been in a claiming race at all, but Dad has to have this operation, so I entered her, and Rodinbaugh—"

"Wait a minute," said Jonas Black, waving his hand wildly. "You had better begin at the beginning. I haven't the least idea what you're talking about!"

Chapter V

Monty and the jockey Irv Blaise had watched Bonnie work out during the morning, and agreed with each other that she seemed in top shape. She was entered in the fourth race that day. It was Irv's considered opinion that she'd win it at a breeze. "That horse is all horse, Monty," asserted the little man, adding as an afterthought, "and all heart, too."

"I wish Julie'd get back from New York." They were walking back to the shed row now. "She probably went up there expecting to work some sort of miracle. I hope she's okay."

"She strikes me as a girl who can handle herself all right," said Irv. "Who knows, maybe she did work a miracle. Charmed old Black out of his boots, I bet."

"That wouldn't get Bonnie back, though. What I hope is that she uncovered some skulduggery. I expected to hear from her by now."

The afternoon replaced the morning; the first and second races were run; and no word came from Julie.

The third race was being called when Julie drove through the gates and parked her car on the lot near the shed row. She went first to the stalls of the Deepwater entries, where she discovered that Dunt Esk was running in this race and that Monty was somewhere in the stands, waiting to see Irv ride her home. By luck she ran into Max McGraw, who told her that Bonnie was entered in the fourth.

"But she mustn't run!" Julie exclaimed.

"Why?"

46

"Because she doesn't belong to that man! She still belongs to me! And for all I know, she isn't ready for another race, and maybe she won't be ridden right, and—"

"Tell me later," Max broke in hastily. "Let's see if we can find Monty." They ran toward the grandstand together.

They located the young trainer within a couple of minutes; on the watch for her, he had seen her towing Max across the nursery course, and recognized her by the long bright hair and the brisk stride that said she was in a hurry.

"Monty! She's still ours!"

"What?" he roared at her. "You did it!"

"We have to stop her from running in this race—"

"She's not in this one," howled Monty over the blast of crowd-noise as the gate flew open and the third race began. "She's in the fourth."

"Well, whatever! I don't want her to run, Monty, with some strange jockey and in the wrong colors and—"

"Go see the stewards," yelled Max McGraw into their ears. "They'll withdraw her."

"Right," screeched Julie with relief.

They found two of the track stewards and poured out the story to them; after consulting with each other at what seemed incredible length, these gentlemen suggested that they could only act on such an unusual situation in the absence of the Racing Secretary, and since he was not absent . . .

Monty and Julie dashed off into the maze of corridors and offices. Jack Lillie wasn't in his office. His secretary was persuaded to put a call for him on the public address system, after much argument. Monty began to teach Julie how to pace back and forth in a three-pace office. At last the secretary appeared.

"This had better be important, Everett," he said darkly. "You can't just go paging me every time you—"

"The claim for Sunbonnet," Julie burst out impetuously, "it's a fake!"

"Can you prove it?" demanded Lillie, his eyes opening wide.

"Here. Mr. Black wrote this out for me this morning." She handed him a damp sheet of paper, which she'd been clutching firmly ever since her arrival at Kandahar. It stated that Jonas Black had never heard of Sunbonnet before now, and had never authorized his trainer Mr. Rodinbaugh to put in a claim for her in his name; in short, that the claim was an out-and-out fraud. "Is that enough?" Julie said huskily.

"More than enough. I think someone's going to lose their trainer's license for life—say, your filly's entered in the next race," he exclaimed.

"We know! Can't she be withdrawn?" Julie asked. "I have the most awful feeling about it."

"She'll have to be." Jack Lillie picked up his phone. "Get me—" Then he lifted his head and listened.

In the distance, through the series of open doors, they could hear the loudspeakers announcing the sounding of the call to the post. "Oh, brother," said Lillie. "Let's try running, shall we?" And they ran.

Fate was determined to beset them with obstacles. They collided with people at corners; Monty tripped on a flight of steps and was saved only by clutching at Lillie and almost bringing him down too; a thick mob of spectators barred them from a quick exit from the grandstand. The horses were in the gate. Surely one of them would misbehave, kick up its heels, rear, try to back out, do something to hold up the start?

Jack Lillie had outdistanced the others and now came to the rail a few yards behind the starting gate. Frantically he waved his arms and shouted at the starter. From his perch high above the gate, the starter waved back cheerfully. Then he looked down, saw that the perfect instant had come, and pushed his button; the doors flew open, the bell clanged, and nine horses broke from the gate in a flying burst of color, to the shouts of the jockeys and the swelling clamor from the grandstand. Jack Lillie relaxed, rather like a puppet whose strings had been snipped, and leaning on the rail, waited for Monty and the girl to find him. Bonnie and the other horses receded down the track and around the clubhouse turn.

"We didn't make it," said Julie, panting in the

Racing Secretary's ear. "She's running, isn't she?"

"She is. Let's go up on the tower and watch." He led them across the track to the starter's perch and one by one they mounted to the point of vantage.

Bonnie was running well, and halfway down the backstretch had already managed to get her nose out in front of the other three leaders. Monty gave Julie his field glasses, and she watched, breathless, as the big bay filly pounded into the far turn, gradually distancing all her competition. At the quarter pole she was an easy two lengths ahead. Then her jockey went to the bat, which is the short whip that each rider carries in a race.

Julie could not believe her eyes. Then Monty behind her said in a loud, incredulous voice, "What's he hitting her for? She's running her heart out for him!"

Bonnie, undoubtedly confused by the sting of the bat, opened another length, then a fourth, between herself and the nearest rival. The crowd-noise was absolute thunder without a letup.

"He's not stopping—he's still hitting her! Monty, he's got no *reason* to hit her! Make him stop!"

"He's just bat-happy," growled Monty, in no position to do anything about the jockey, and seething with anger. Jack Lillie had gone down the ladder and was making his way quickly toward the nearest phone that connected with the administration building. Julie bounced up and down with near-panic, losing Bonnie in the glasses and then finding her again. As the whip flailed and flailed, Bonnie came down and crossed the wire five and a half lengths ahead of the second horse.

"Well, she won," said Monty, "no thanks to that jerk in the saddle."

"If she's hurt—"

"She isn't. But I'll bet she's really baffled, poor thing. She's never been hit before, not with anything."

"Let's go and collect her," said Julie, scrambling down the ladder and heading for the winner's circle.

The public address system cautioned all patrons to hold onto their tickets, as there was some question about the fourth race.

"Why?" demanded Julie, as they hurried along. "She won it fair and square, even if he *did* wallop her."

"She'll be disqualified. She was run under an entry that contained at least one misstatement: her ownership."

"You mean she won't collect all that money, after going like—like an east wind in Ohio in November?"

"No. Rules of racing, Julie. She belongs to you, but she was entered by Rodinbaugh for Black, who has no claim on her at all."

"Then the whole thing was really useless. And all that hitting. Oh, I could just simply swear at that man," said Julie passionately.

"Personally, I'd like to knock his head against his jockey's a couple of times," agreed Monty. "They're a real pair, those two."

Bonnie was ridden into the winner's circle; a steward spoke quietly to the jockey, who popped his eyes in disbelief and slowly dismounted. Julie came into the small enclosure and could not stifle a cry of joy as she put her hand tenderly on the sweating shoulder. Bonnie nuzzled her as though they had not been separated for more than a few minutes. The jockey, without looking at any of them, took the gear off the horse and disappeared. Monty put a halter on her.

"Miss Jefferson, will you go up to the Racing Secretary's office at once, please?" said the steward.

"I have to see she gets back to her stall and—"

"I'll take care of her," said Monty. "Go on, Julie."

"Oh. Okay." The loudspeakers blared impersonally, "Number Seven in the fourth race, Sunbonnet, has been disqualified for technical fraud by reason of entry misstatement," and a thousand wails went up from disappointed bettors. Julie walked slowly out of the enclosure and headed for Jack Lillie's headquarters.

Rodinbaugh was there just before her, his face nearly black with rage. "What's all that guff about disqualified for fraud?" he shouted hoarsely at the Racing Secretary, leaning over his desk. "What fraud? I demand—"

"You aren't in a position to demand anything," said Lillie evenly. "Suppose you tell me about the claim you registered for Miss Jefferson's horse yesterday. Come in, Miss Jefferson, do sit down."

Julie sat on the edge of a chair, glaring at the tall man in the Stetson, who gave her an evil glance and turned his back on her.

"What about it? Isn't Jonas Black's name good enough for you?"

"As good as anyone's, if it's backed up by his own word."

"What are you talking about?"

"Didn't you know the truth would come out? What got into you, Rodinbaugh? Didn't you figure out that you'd lose your license for good? How long have you held it?"

"Fourteen years. I demand—"

"I tell you, you can't demand anything. Lower your voice." The genial Jack Lillie, who Julie had grown to like, was as grim and threatening as Rodinbaugh himself, but a lot less blustering. "Are you going to tell me what kind of stupid idea you had in your head when you registered a claim in the name of your boss, who didn't even know of the horse you were claiming?" He waved the paper that Julie had brought from New York. "Don't tell me you didn't realize that the facts would come out?"

"What facts, blast you?"

Two of the stewards came into the office and shut the door behind them. Rodinbaugh stared around him like a wild beast at his enemies closing for the kill.

"If you had any reason whatever for perpetrating this hoax, Rodinbaugh," said Lillie, "you'd better tell it to us now. Otherwise I will recommend strongly that your license be revoked and that you be barred from the track."

"Suppose you tell me what you're talking about. What's that paper?"

"A letter from Black, in his own handwriting, denying all knowledge of both the filly and the claim on her in his name. It furthermore stipulates that you have no authorization to make any claim for him without his approval."

"Where'd you get a thing like that?" Rodinbaugh shouted.

"I got it from Mr. Black," said Julie, noticing with a little embarrassment that her voice was shaking. The tall man was frightening, as frightening as the crook Alex Homer, whom she'd fought over Bonnie. His light eyes were absolutely insane as he gazed back at her.

"You little . . . I want to talk to Jonas Black," he said between set teeth.

"Sorry, that's unnecessary and impossible. The facts speak for themselves. Did you actually believe," Lillie asked him, as comprehension of the notion that might have been in Rodinbaugh's mind occurred to both the Racing Secretary and Julie herself at the same moment, "that you could claim a horse and then persuade Black to agree to buying her? Did you think he'd back you in your claim? That maybe you could persuade him to sell her to you afterwards? Good heavens, what sort of man did you think you were working for?"

"I'm not talking till I see my lawyer."

"See him, then. Meanwhile, I want you off Kandahar in an hour."

"Don't worry, I will be," he said, sneering.

A steward made a last attempt to reason with him. "Rodinbaugh, I've known you a long time. You're no fool. If this was some sort of plot to get hold of a potential high-stakes winner, and there were others in it with you—"

"I should tell you their names and you'll see that it goes easy for me," finished Rodinbaugh, laughing coldly. "Don't get melodramatic, Jackson. I just put in a claim for my boss and now he decides he doesn't want the nag, so he'll ditch her and let me take the blame. Okay. That's it. Are you through with me, Lillie?"

"Yes. Get out. I'm sorry to say that I consider you a disgrace to an honest sport," said Jack Lillie wearily.

"You haven't heard the last of me, you meddling brat," said the tall man to Julie, settling his big hat down over the bridge of his nose.

"That's enough!" shouted Lillie angrily. "I'll report that last crack to the police, Rodinbaugh, and that's no idle threat."

"Report away, you bubblehead," said Rodinbaugh, and went out of the room with a swagger.

"A mean customer," said one of the stewards.

"He's all talk," said the other. "Don't fret over him, Miss Jefferson."

"Thanks. I'll try not to," said Julie, who felt scared. She was not used to people making sinister warnings in her direction. "Are there many men like him in racing? Because I seem to have met three of them already, and—"

"I've been in the game for thirty years, and he's the first I've met," said Jackson comfortingly. "And he's all talk, really. He's only rattled because his plans fell through and he's lost his job."

"There are bad dogs in every big pack, as my mother used to say," Lillie told her, smiling. "I think you've probably met your quota for a lifetime."

"I hope so," said Julie fervently. "What about Bonnie, now—will I have to sign papers and things?"

"I don't think so. If you do, I'll mail them to you. As far as I'm concerned, she always was yours, and it's too bad she had to run that race when her fine performance didn't count. You go on back home with her whenever you like. And I hope we'll be seeing more of both of you at Kandahar Park."

"I'm sure you will. Thank you so much for everything you've done," said Julie, and shook hands all around and left them. All the way to the shed row she watched for a tall man in a Stetson, but saw nothing of him anywhere. Monty greeted her with a half a dozen questions before she could even ask him where Bonnie was.

"Oh, Irv's cooling her out himself. He's as glad to have her back as we are, I believe. What about Rodinbaugh?"

"He's suspended, and barred from Kandahar, and he'll lose his trainer's license and I don't know, maybe even go to jail, because he threatened me."

"What did he say?" demanded Monty instantly.

"Just that I hadn't seen the last of him."

"Well, he won't go to jail for that. That's just words. Now you aren't to worry, Julie."

"Okay, I'm not. I was spooked for a minute, I admit. He looks so tough, and he wouldn't explain anything about the claim."

"I figure he heard about her somehow, and thought he could buy her in Black's name and then buy her himself, from Black, and—"

"Yes, but it seems pretty dumb, doesn't it, for anyone who's been around racing as long as he has? He says he's been a trainer for fourteen years."

"I bet he's tied up with Matthews or Homer. Well, it doesn't matter now. It's over, and you have Bonnie back."

"Yes. And I'll never enter her in a claiming race again, not if she was to bring a million dollars!"

Chapter VI

Rand Jefferson was operated upon three days later. Rollin Tolkov insisted that Julie go home to be near him and to nurse him back to health. Mr. T was going to Europe on business, or, he assured her, he would have gone up to Blankton himself, just to meet the man who was her father. "Because he sounds like quite a fellow."

"He is," said Julie.

"And Julie," said Mr. T, "it might be a good idea if you were to take Bonnie home with you."

"Why? You think she's in danger, don't you?"

"No, not really. I believe that this was the last attempt anyone will make to acquire her, by fair means or foul; her story is spreading now, you can bet, and there's no reason why it shouldn't. Horses that are owned legitimately and raced under their owners' colors are *not* in constant peril of being stolen, or having other horses substituted for them, despite your experience so far this year—Bonnie's history is just about unique in the game, I'd say. So you aren't to lose any more sleep about her, my dear."

"Still, you think I ought to take her to St. Clair with me, as a precaution," Julie said quietly.

"No, not as a precaution; though I admit I'll feel better when Jack Lillie has discovered what sort of idea this Rodinbaugh had in his head when he claimed her spuriously. But I think you ought to take her along because you'd both be happier if you were together."

"Well, that's true, goodness knows."

"And Monty can decide when she ought to start racing again. He'll be joining you for the Christmas season, I'm sure."

"Mr. T," she asked, cocking her head at him, "are all millionaire bosses as nice as you?"

"Every one," he said solemnly. "We are the salt of the earth."

So she drove north to Ohio, to the St. Clair Farm near Blankton, and behind her car in a small two-horse trailer came the great racing filly Sunbonnet; and Julie drove as carefully as if she had been hauling nine hundred pounds of eggshell porcelain.

She was greeted warmly by her old buddy, Stash Watkins, the head groom at St. Clair, and abruptly (that was his way) by Will Everett, Monty's father, the foreman; she also met Stash's oldest son, Beau, for the first time in a couple of years, and at last was able to thank him enthusiastically for his good care of her father.

Beau was a short, slight, wiry young man, obviously intended for a jockey from his birth, who loved horses as much as Julie did and knew almost as much about them as Stash himself. He stabled Bonnie and walked around her several times, clucking his tongue. "Some lot of horse, Miss Jefferson. I knew she cost a fortune, and had terrific bloodlines, and won her first race practically walkin', but nobody told me she was the prettiest filly in the profession," he said, thus winning a friend for life.

Julie beamed at him.

"Sure hope I can ride her some day. In a big race."

"So do I. Who are you riding for now, Beau?"

"Nobody. I'm at liberty. My boss retired and broke up his stable."

"Beau has his jockey's license now," said Stash, barely smothering his pride at the fact. "Lookin' for a berth with some good big stable."

"I'll ask Mr. T if Deepwater needs another jockey. It would be nice to have you with us, Beau. Like old-home week all the time, with three St. Clair people down there," Julie told him. "And I'm sure Bonnie would love you to ride her."

"She *loves* you to ride her, Julie," corrected Stash; "she would *put up with* anybody else."

Bonnie whickered her agreement.

Julie went out to unhitch the trailer and drive over to her father's house. Stash and Beau watched her go. "Son, you keep an eye on this little mare any time you ain't up to the eyebrows in other work, you hear me?"

"Sure, Pop. How come?"

"She's had enough trouble 'n' strife for any one horse. You know about that. Our job's seein' she doesn't collect any more."

"Danger of that?"

"Don't just know. But Mr. Monty he called me up this mornin' and tells me to skin my eyes for strangers while she's here, 'specially a tall rapscallion with pale winkers in a brown face, dressed like he's headin' for the OK Corral."

"Rodinbaugh," said Beau promptly. "Trainer for Mr. Black."

"*Ex*-trainer. Know him?"

"Seen him around tracks. He never impressed me as much."

"Mr. Monty didn't say, but I figure he's lookin' to cause Julie and Bonnie mischief; and we don't stand for that, son."

"Right."

"Now give this fine girl an apple and we get back to work."

Rand Jefferson was brought home a few days later, pale beneath the remains of his suntan and very weak, but in his usual jaunty spirits. Burglar, the raccoon, immediately took up residence on his bed, and the two retrievers, Cissy and Joey, posted themselves at either side of it. Julie devoted herself to caring for him and, after the first twenty-four hours, trying vainly to make him rest what she considered long enough at a time.

"My joints will rust up if I don't move around, Julie. Doctor said I was to exercise."

"Yes, but sensibly! Oh, dear."

So to keep him quiet she talked to him, hour after hour, telling him with all the detail she could remember of Bonnie's first and second races, of the Blacks, Rodinbaugh, Deepwater Farm, and her job, so that he knew eventually almost as much as she did about the past weeks in Kentucky. After that, they talked of what he would do when he could get around once more; of Kitty, who was running Rand's antique shop with easy efficiency; and of Bonnie, who was on the road that would lead, Julie was sure of it, to the great Triple Crown—the Kentucky Derby, the Preakness, and the Belmont Stakes.

"That's pretty high aiming, honey."

"Oh, I know you think I'm building myself up to an awful letdown, Dad, but I'm not. She's good enough, honest, and by the time May is here, she'll be ready. I talked to Mr. T about it. He's on my side."

"Well, so am I, you know that; but if she doesn't make it—"

"Dad, I'm able to handle disappointment."

He smiled up at her. "Yes, I think you are. Okay, I'll start saving my nickels so I can lay a bet on her in each race."

"You won't lose, either. Oh, you should *see* her fly!"

"I'm anxious to. Maybe by New Year's Day I'll be able to get over to St. Clair to watch her."

But Christmas brought not only Monty from Kentucky but also a heavy layer of snow from the north; and when more inches were added to it each day, it became obvious that the big outdoor track at St. Clair's would not be used for quite a while. By then, Rand was getting from room to room with a minimum of pain, and yearning to be outside again. Julie bundled him up like an overdressed panda in numerous layers of coats and sweaters, and drove him carefully to the St. Clair stable for a mildly festive New Year's Eve party that was held in the big tack room, where Stash had had his men bring every comfortable chair available. They drank cider and nibbled cookies and talked in the cozy, horse-and-leather-smelling atmosphere, and the talk was all of horses: of how this one had won a fine race against incredible odds, and that one had lost by a whisker, and the other had run its heart out for what Will Everett, uncharacteristically sentimental at this season, referred to as a distinct moral victory. The talk was of giant horses of the past, of not-bad horses of the present, and of sensational horses yet to appear on the racing scene. The talk was, at last, of Bonnie; and Monty and Julie took turns interrupting each other to tell them all of the claiming race in which the magnificent bay, boxed and banged in the pack until the far turn, had come round on the outside and blazed to the winner's position. Stash's eyes glowed with pride, and Beau absolutely wriggled at the thought of riding her.

"When will she run again, Julie?" asked Will.

"Gosh, I don't know. The way she goes around the indoor ring, I think she wants to race every day. But it's up to Monty." They all turned to stare at Monty. "Mr. T said he'd leave it up to you," Julie said.

"Yes. Well, I had a letter from him today. He's in France, and may be back in a month or not, depending on business." Monty dug an envelope from his inside pocket. "He says—where is it—'About Julie's Bonnie, if you think she's ready, I suggest you enter her in the Forget-Me-Not Stakes at Hialeah—' "

"That's a rich race," said Stash, "but it's kinda late to be tryin' for an entry."

" 'I will be glad to take care of her nomination fee, as well as the penalty for late entry,' " Monty finished.

"You? Where would you get that kind of money?" demanded his father, with a mouth full of cookie.

"Not me, Dad. Mr. Tolkov."

"Oh. Well, he can afford it, I guess. He must think a lot of that filly."

"He paid four hundred thousand dollars for her," said Monty mildly.

"Dad paid two hundred dollars for her, which is more, really, in proportion," said Julie loyally.

"Which Julie has already paid back," added Rand. "With about a thousand percent interest. Sunbonnet's earning her price and keep."

"She'll do it for Mr. T, too. He and I are going to share in her foals," Julie told them. "Monty, let's put her in for the Forget-Me-Not!"

"I'll wire them tomorrow. It's run in mid-February. That's time and to spare for getting her down to Florida and putting her in top-notch form." He put a hand on Julie's shoulder. "How soon do you think you can leave for the sunny Southland?"

Julie thought quickly of several possibilities. Then she turned to her father. "How soon could *you* travel, Dad?"

"Oh, if I were going anywhere, I'd guess about a week. But not by car, kitten; as far as that, I'd have to fly. You need my expert help in the finer points of training her?" he asked, grinning. He was the only soul there who was not actively engaged in the business of raising and training racehorses, and was kidding himself, so they all chuckled. Except Julie.

"You need my expert help in getting better. The warm climate will be good for you; don't think I don't realize how the cold bites into that awful wound!"

"It's not a wound, it's progressing toward a state of scardom quite nicely."

"You know what I mean, anyway. The heat will improve it, I bet."

"Right," said Stash. "As one old vet'rinary to another, Mr. Jefferson, she's abso-tively on the nose about that. Nothin' like heat to sop up the pangs."

"And Bonnie owes you a vacation, Dad. In fact, she owes you her life."

"She's more than repaid me, Julie. I can't go down there and be a burden to you, with Bonnie in such a big race and your hands full enough—"

Will Everett snapped out, "Randolph Jefferson, you old stove-up bull-headed coot, you haven't been a burden to anybody since you were two years old! Go on down to Florida. I'll see that your dogs are pampered in their usual style, dang it. I'll even bed down that idiot raccoon for you."

"Will, you've been trying to get Burglar away from me ever since he climbed on your lap last October!"

"I wouldn't have your menagerie for all the liniment in Lima, Peru, except to force you into getting some sunshine! It'll be an awful chore, I'm telling you, but I'll do it."

"So you'll come down," said Julie, very grateful.

"I'll come down," said Rand. "With many thanks."

Monty rubbed his jaw thoughtfully. "All my men are going to be busy for two months," he said, and sipped cider, and looked at Julie hard. "I've been planning things, ever since this letter came, and here's the way it stands: I'll take eighteen or nineteen of the Deepwater horses to Florida, plus Bonnie. There'll be you and Dan Gibson and myself, but the other exercise boys and apprentices are spoken for elsewhere. I'll need one more good hand."

Julie looked over at Stash's son, sitting in the corner. "Beau," she said.

"I had Beau in mind. I'll take the responsibility of hiring him, at least on a temporary basis, because I need him badly. Mr. T will understand." He swiveled toward Beau. "Would you come?"

"Mr. Monty," said Beau, "you're in luck. It just happens that I'm at liberty." He gave Julie a slow wink.

"Out of sight!" said Julie happily.

Chapter VII

They had been settled in Florida for nearly a week. Rand was improving so fast that Monty swore he could *see* him getting better. The five human members of the Deepwater team lived at the Martingale, an almost new motel within easy distance of Hialeah Park. The twenty horses were accommodated at the track.

As a result of her three-week rest at St. Clair, Bonnie was looking her best. Julie had not detected a single bad effect of the stupid ride she had been given in her second race; afraid at first that the unaccustomed batting might have produced a nervousness where human beings were concerned—he had known it to happen like that, Stash had told her somberly, when a horse had never felt a whip till it was two or three, and then had felt it for little or no reason—Julie was now reassured that Bonnie's horse-sense had shrugged it all off as something of no importance. "Like her first sight of a raccoon," she told Monty. "It was awful, but it doesn't worry her any more."

So Bonnie, with Julie up, was exercised every day at the splendid big track at Hialeah, and grew used to the long-legged flamingos that lived on the infield.

There came a morning when Monty, frowning thoughtfully, watched Julie adjusting the six-pound exercise saddle—the leathercovered felt pad that was "just something to hang your irons on"—on Bonnie, and said, "It's time Beau started doing this job, Julie; he'll be riding her and they ought to get used to each other soon, as much so as you and she are."

"Right. Why don't you work her out now, Beau?"

"Glad to. Been wantin' to get really acquainted with this fine filly."

He had a way with horses, Beau Watkins had, and Julie felt even less concern about his riding Bonnie than she had felt about the old hand, Irv Blaise. Julie herself mounted Curious Cottabus, the big brown gelding, and Dan Gibson, Monty's other assistant, got up on Gramarye, a bay. Monty was riding the brown-and-white work pony.

Any animal that leads a horse at the track is called a "pony," although a *real* pony is never more than fourteen-two hands high. The main requirement for a work pony is that it must not kick; and of course it must be a tough beast, going, as it does, as much as fifteen or twenty miles in a day at a near-gallop. This one was a gelding named Ginger, fifteen hands high and hard as a horse made of wire.

Riding Ginger and holding the shank that kept Bonnie's head at his knee, Monty led them out onto the track and turned right along the outside rail where etiquette demands that the slower horses work. They jogged some distance to loosen their muscles, then lifted into a gallop for a good mile, Bonnie's head held steady beside Monty.

"All right," Monty said, as they galloped along, "the three of you work a mile. Then turn in."

He leaned down and unsnapped the lead rope from Bonnie's bridle, barely slowing Ginger's gait as the trio drew away from him.

Scarcely had the three riders begun urging their mounts into movement when, Bonnie without any warning dropped her shoulder, humped violently, leaped sideways, and hurled Beau off her back. Whinnying loudly, she then took off, and in spite of Julie's shouted commands to come back this minute, never slowed down until she had arrived at the barn.

"Go on with your work," Monty told the others. "Beau, you all right?"

"Sure. Injured dignity, that's all. What for would she do a stunt like that? I thought we were pals," said Beau, slapping dirt from his pants.

"Let's go back and see if she's okay."

"I'll come too," said Julie anxiously.

"You'll finish your work with the Cottabus, Julie."

"But Bonnie—"

"Bonnie is perfectly fine," Monty told her in a low tone that didn't carry to Beau and Dan. "Either you have a job working for me, or you're down here to nurse that filly day and night, in which case I'll have to take you off Mr. T's payroll. Which is it going to be, Julie?"

"You're being *mean*."

"I am not. But this is a good time for you to decide between doing Mr. T's work and devoting all your hours to your own horse. I'm sorry," he said flatly, "that's the way it's got to be."

They glared at each other for a moment. Then gradually it dawned on Julie that he was quite right. She had kept Bonnie in her thoughts, first and foremost, from the day she came to work for Mr. T; and Monty had allowed her to do it until now, probably because she was still very young, it was her first real job, and Bonnie had been such a source of worry and fear for her. But it had to end. He was right about that. She couldn't go flying off to her filly's side, leaving others to do double work, every time Bonnie sneezed or stamped hard or—or threw a rider. She had to stop believing that Bonnie was made out of tissue paper and gold leaf that only she, Julie, could hold together in the shape of a horse!

She grinned at her friend. "Lesson One inhaled and understood by the whole class, sir," she said, saluting in a well-meaning but rather awkward fashion. "Carry on."

"Attagirl." He was proud of her, prouder than usual.

"But be sure there isn't a burr under her saddle," Julie said, wheeling the Cottabus out into line with Gramarye.

"A woman always has the last word," said Beau from the collected wisdom of his twenty years. "You got to acknowledge that if you're goin' to work with one."

"Right on," said Monty, chuckling. "Let's go take a look at the other skittish female."

Bonnie proved to be perfectly sound, no burrs, no sore back, no leg swollen, no shoe loose, nothing whatever wrong. She accepted a carrot from Beau and even kissed him on the cheek with her soft upper lip. Some of the other exercise boys had come over to see that she was in satisfactory condition, for Bonnie had a growing reputation as an absolute lamb on the track.

"You mean this gentle critter dumped a genuine jockey onto the track? This meek li'l filly that lets a *girl* ride her every day?"

"Hard to believe, isn't it? She gallops with a girl, but throws a man. You think maybe he just leaned over to pick up the reins and *fell* off?"

"Well, I heard that he didn't know she was gonna start right then, and he didn't move forward when she did, so he slid right over her tail."

"Maybe we ought to take up a collection 'n' buy him a riding lesson."

And a lot more of the same. Beau brought the teasing to an end by saying soberly, "The glue in the saddle didn't hold. I got me some stronger stuff ordered."

Three days later when Monty was ready to work her again, he once more gave Beau the mount. This time he decided to pony her first for a mile-long gallop and then send her alone to breeze—that is, work at a restrained racing pace—for five furlongs. Bonnie showed no sign of displeasure as they walked out onto the track, and did her mile's gallop in good order. Monty did not think twice about leaning over, unsnapping the lead rope, and dropping back to watch; but no sooner had Ginger disappeared from her side than Bonnie wheeled uncontrollably, pitched her rider off over her head with a real western-style buck and twist, and bolted from the track.

Julie was in the stable area, cooling out the little mare Fancy, when Sunbonnet came clattering in at a gallop, her nostrils cracking and her head flung high. Monty was right behind her on Ginger. Julie calmly unsaddled her and put her into her stall, then started to go over her with gently probing fingers, soothing her with quiet talk and loving pats. Bonnie settled down quickly. Beau came limping in, shamefaced, and paying no heed to an ankle that was already swelling. He was concerned only with the filly's welfare. "Is she okay? Is she?" It was no laughing matter this time: *twice* could not be explained as coincidence or sudden fright at something she'd seen; *twice* was serious.

"She isn't hurt," said Julie.

"But you are," Monty said to his jockey. "Let's see that ankle."

"Just twisted it. Tape it up, it'll be great. Why's that girl chuck me off, anyway? Give me a piece o' sugar." He brought it over and Bonnie accepted it leisurely. "See? She got nothing against me. What's the matter?"

"I don't understand it, I confess." Monty scratched his jaw. "She likes you fine."

He taped up the twisted ankle, which Beau swore was nothing to excite himself about. Hesitantly, Julie leaned over the stall door and said, "Could it be that when she ran her second race, that bat-happy jockey scared her worse than we think? Could she be afraid of having a man in the saddle?"

"I don't know. It's pretty farfetched."

"But it's what she acts like. The minute you're not there holding her with a rope, she goes wild. Unless I'm up. Maybe she thinks she's going to be shipped again."

"If she does, she sure doesn't hold any grudge afterwards," said Beau, giving her another sugar lump. "I could sleep in this stall and she wouldn't hurt me."

"Suppose I exercise her tomorrow," Julie suggested. "In the same way, with Ginger beside her, and the rope. If she tries to throw me, I'll be ready. But I'll bet you a dollar that she won't."

Monty agreed to try this. There was nothing else he could think of to try, anyway.

That afternoon Julie was called to the office of the track stewards and given a thorough, stern talking-to concerning Bonnie's unseating of Beau. The safety that was a major requirement at the track was brought up; the barring of a consistently vicious horse was mentioned. . . .

"But she isn't any more vicious than a puppy!" said Julie hotly.

"She's balked twice at running under a jockey with a good reputation. She hasn't stepped on him, I agree, but she could have broken his neck. A horse that does that can't be allowed to run at Hialeah, any more than it can anywhere else in the country, Miss Jefferson."

Wishing that this stern stranger were Jack Lillie, so that she might pour out her worry and wonder at Bonnie's baffling behavior, Julie apologized for the horse and said that they were watching her carefully.

"So are we. Don't forget it. If she throws anyone again, she's out of the Forget-Me-Not."

"Yes, sir. Thank you, sir." Julie made her escape, breathing hard and wondering how she could convince the stewards that her Bonnie was as gentle as a fawn. If she threw Beau once more, well—

"No way," said Julie aloud, "no way at all."

Chapter VIII

Dawnlight on a warm morning, and Julie told herself as they rode at a jog around the track that even here, miles away from it, she could swear that she smelled the saltness of the sea.

Monty had deliberately planned a "daylight" work; not as an attempt to work the horse before the clockers arrived, which is the customary reason for it, nor to avoid the watchful glare of the stewards, but to ensure Julie's safety on the deserted track in case Bonnie gave another of her Wild West broncho performances. Beau, whose well-taped ankle was giving him little trouble, was on the swift little chestnut Bandicoot beside them.

"Same as yesterday," said Monty loudly in the hush of the world's wakening. "I'll unsnap her after a mile of galloping, and you two breeze for five furlongs. Beau, stay well off to the side, but let Bonnie see you there all the time. Let's go."

The gallop went well. Then Monty had freed her of the rope, and Julie was far forward and urging her on, and Bonnie streaked into a powerful, easy breeze that had Bandicoot working hard to match. The wind of their own making was sharp in her face and Julie felt again the glorious, free sensation of diving headlong through thin fresh clouds that she so often experienced on the back of this great driving animal—*as though she were really the winged horse,* she thought, delighted. And Bonnie had suddenly taken the initiative and shot forward ahead of the chestnut, but slowed at once (Julie could not be sure whether it was her own pull on the reins, or the filly's own desire); then they had gone the five furlongs and more, and Julie stood up in her irons to pull up. They trotted back to Monty.

"No sign of balkiness?"

"None at all." Julie smiled at Beau. "Sorry, she *does* like you—"

"But not in the saddle," finished Beau ruefully. "Man, though, can't she run! I tried to stay head and head, and she just wouldn't let me, there at the end."

But I think she did let you, Julie thought; I think she eased up when she couldn't see Bandicoot. I'm not certain, but I believe . . .

She said nothing about it aloud, however, because she was not sure enough of it to make an issue for them to fret over.

"Julie, you work her this week," Monty said as they went back to collect Dan and three of the other horses for another workout. "Maybe it was the whipping, and maybe in a few days she'll have forgotten about it. I don't know anything else to try."

That evening he called Leon Pitt, who knew horses as well as any man alive, and talked it over with him. But the old hand could come up with nothing that Monty had not already thought of, except that Beau must spend all his spare time befriending Bonnie, and "be sure he keeps plenty of gumdrops in his pockets for her. Nobody but Beau's to give her that favorite treat, not even Julie. Maybe that'll do a little good. I truly don't know."

Beau followed orders, and Bonnie got into the habit of watching for him. To all appearances they were the closest pals on the track. Some days later, therefore, Monty tried him out as her rider once more.

And Bonnie put on the same display for them. Luckily, it was another dawn ride, and no one witnessed the scene except their own people. But this time Bonnie, in her skittish leaping to unseat Beau—which she did not manage to do—as soon as he had taken her out ahead of the work pony, crashed against the outer guard rail and cut her foreleg. It was not a bad wound, and needed only an application of Furacin ointment and a small bandage, but it forced Monty to recognize a cold, dismal fact.

"She won't run for anyone but you, Julie. If she would, it would certainly be Beau, because she adores him. But when he's in the saddle he isn't Beau, he's a *man,* and it was a man who walloped her. I guess we have to admit that. He spoiled her for any rider but you."

"What on earth will we *do,* Monty?"

"The only thing we can do. Apply for a jockey's license for you."

"Me! I'm a girl. I'm seventeen. I'm—"

"You're a terrific rider. After all, a girl rode in the Kentucky Derby not long ago, the first ever. They can't deny you a license for that reason."

"Me in a big stakes race. Oh wow," said Julie, breathless.

But not frightened. She thought about it for ten solid minutes before she concluded that. She wasn't at all afraid to do it, not with Bonnie under her. She and Bonnie were a team. Suddenly it seemed quite logical.

"Okay. What do we do?" she asked. By this time she was jogging Curious Cottabus around the track beside Monty and Beau and Dan Gibson. "Where do we start?"

"By submitting your application. We'll see about it this afternoon."

Monty had more to worry over than Julie and Bonnie, and he was about to be handed another source of anxiety. From the time they had arrived in Florida, Dan Gibson had been far from his usual pleasant, efficient self. He had something on his mind that was making him progressively more jumpy and inclined to carelessness, and Monty could not persuade him to talk about it. Only yesterday he had nearly run Fancy into the filly Dunt Esk, purely because he was obviously miles away, and absentminded beyond tolerance. Monty had chewed him out bitterly, but still he wouldn't say what was gnawing at him. Ever since then, Monty had kept an eye on him anxiously; now he saw Dan staring down the track with a deep crease between his eyes and his lower lip between his teeth. Monty looked quickly in that direction.

He was just in time to see a man turn and leave the rail, and disappear among the buildings near the grandstand. He could not have sworn to the fellow's identity, but he was tall and moved in an easy, loose-jointed way. And he was wearing a broadbrimmed hat.

What was Rodinbaugh doing at Hialeah, weeks before the next races were to be run?

Monty groaned inside, and dropping Ginger back, walked him to the rail to watch the other three breeze.

"All I need now," he told the gelding, "is for the Army to call me back. Or for Bonnie to decide that she doesn't want to run for Julie either. Man! Isn't life complicated enough, with twenty horses to coddle? Do I have to have a goofy horse, two distracted assistants, a jockey with a wrenched ankle, and a crooked trainer spying on me?"

Ginger snorted with sympathy. A cloud moved over the sun, and it started to look like rain.

That afternoon the two of them went to the proper office and filled out all the necessary forms to apply for Julie's license as a jockey. A problem came up when Monty discovered something that he'd known but forgotten: she needed a second trainer's signature (his was the first). "Wait here," he said, and taking the paper, dashed out to the stable area.

Up and down the shed row he went until he found Jimmy Mohler, a friend of his, who now worked for Jonas Black; he had taken the place of Rodinbaugh.

At first Jimmy was reluctant. "I've seen her on her filly, sure, but I don't know——"

"Is my word good enough for you? I tell you, she can ride as well as you can. And she isn't going public." (To go public is to make oneself available for hire.) "She works for Tolkov and she'll never ride for anyone else. In fact, she'll never ride any animal but Sunbonnet, you can bet on that. This is an emergency. Sign the blasted thing."

"Okay, if you say she's that good, I'll endorse her.

You sweet on her?" asked Jimmy, smiling at him. "She's mighty pretty, I admit."

"We're old friends. Knew each other when we were kids," Monty growled.

"That's why you're blushing."

"I always blush when it's hot. I haven't stopped blushing since I hit Florida. Thanks, Jimmy," he said, grabbing the paper back. "I'll do you a favor some day."

"Introduce me to Julie Jefferson," said Jimmy.

"Go fly up a tree," Monty suggested coolly, and ran back to the offices. The application was so late now, he thought, that every minute counted.

When the application had been filed, Monty gave his various problems some intensive consideration. The best thing to do was to eliminate all of them he could; it wasn't smart to go laboring along under a load of cares, hoping for the best. With all his responsibilities, he had to keep as clear a head as possible.

So he talked to several of the stewards, to find that they knew nothing about Rodinbaugh's losing his license. "But he's not trying to work here, you know," said the second of them. "He's been visiting—I don't know, a friend or a relative, I think. We have no reason to bar him from the track."

"I guess not," nodded Monty glumly. The man had not done anything as dangerous to racing as drugging a horse or attempting to injure one; he'd only put in a false claim, and losing his license was considered punishment enough.

"I'll pass the word for my people to keep an eye on him, that's all I can do," said the steward.

"Thanks," said Monty.

He put in a call to Jack Lillie, up at Kandahar Park. Jack was regretful and understanding. "I'd stew some too, in your place, son. Look, I'll talk to a couple of my friends down there. I think Rodinbaugh's attitude and absolute refusal, even now, to tell the authorities who he was working with and what he had in mind, are ample reason to bar him from any track. I'll talk strong. But I can't promise anything."

That was that, for the present. Monty went and had

another stern talk with Dan Gibson, to see whether he might not be able to clear up *that* problem, and again got nowhere with the distracted, secretive assistant. Then he insisted that Beau have his ankle examined by a doctor, much to Beau's disgust. The doctor said that it was coming along as well as could be expected, but that Beau shouldn't be working a full schedule.

"So now, with all my problems taken care of," said Monty to Julie, his face perfectly blank, "I can relax and get on with my usual work."

"I'm sorry we're causing you so much trouble," she told him seriously. "I'll do anything I can to help, you know that."

"Don't be silly, Julie Jefferson. You aren't causing me trouble."

"Oh yes, we are. Bonnie and I."

"You're the objects of the trouble, not the subjects, if those are the terms I mean. It's only because Bonnie is so fine a horse that everything's happened—Rodinbaugh, before him those two crooks, they'd never have given us any bother at all if she hadn't been so valuable. I don't know what's bugging Dan, but I doubt that it's Bonnie. And the difficulties that Bonnie's creating herself, they can all be laid to Rodinbaugh's door, his and that bat-happy jockey's."

"Well, if it weren't for Bonnie—"

"You wouldn't be working for Mr. T and me. That's worth a little trouble, isn't it?"

"I don't know. Is it?"

"Sure it is! Do you think I'd enjoy having a thousand miles between you and me?"

Julie giggled. "At this moment, I think you'd enjoy that a lot, yes."

"Well, I wouldn't, smart apple. I—you—you're the best friend I have, and it's great to be working with you alongside of me." He scowled at her, embarrassed. "So stop feeling guilty," he said. "We have a lot of work to do."

"Fine. What next?"

"It's time to work the big girl out of the starting gate."

"Shall I saddle her? You want to do it now?"

"Might as well. I'm a little anxious about it."

"You think she might—"

"At this point, I'm not thinking at all. Not in advance. Remember what Stash would say about borrowing trouble, and let's get Bonnie ready."

Now Julie had been far more disturbed over her filly's uncharacteristic behavior than she had let any of the other members of Deepwater Farm's team realize. But ever since Monty's mild lecture had wakened her sense of duty toward her employer, the kind and thoughtful Mr. Tolkov, she had been keeping her emotions strictly to herself. It was the only way in which she could help Monty, and therefore Mr. T. The longer she'd done it, the more deeply she'd understood how just shutting up could contribute a great deal to relieving the tension of a bad situation. It would have been different if she'd *known* something that the others did not; then keeping quiet would have been pretty dumb. But to go around wringing her hands and wailing "What can be the matter?"— which, she admitted to herself, she sometimes had a frantic desire to do—would have added to everybody's troubles.

Especially my own, she said to herself, as she put the saddle across Bonnie's back. Maybe if I learn *that,* bone-deep, then something good will have come out of all this worry and apprehension.

She thought briefly of her father, who was improving rapidly. She suspected that he knew perfectly well how scared she was about the horse. She also suspected that he was rather proud of her for keeping still on the subject. Well, she said inside herself, I had a couple of pretty fair teachers on the matter of growing up: Dad and good old Stash. And now Monty's taking a hand.

Julie was grateful to all three of them, and for an instant felt warm and happy and well protected. Then Bonnie was ready to be ridden out, and Julie stopped being philosophical and got down to business.

There was a lull out on the training track, although it was still afternoon and a number of horses might have been expected to be working out. With Monty beside

her on Ginger, Julie trotted her filly down the homestretch toward the big many-compartmented gate. In
spite of having been ridden that morning, Bonnie
seemed eager for a good hard run, and tossed her head
happily as they approached the starting line. But when
they veered over toward the gate itself, she put back
her ears and would have stopped if Julie hadn't urged
her forward.

"She doesn't want to go into it."

"That's all right, she hasn't been in one for quite a
while," said Monty, watching the big bay sharply. He
dropped back behind her. "Take her in."

Julie headed her for one of the stalls. Bonnie stopped
short and said something in a brief whinny, something
that sounded like a flat refusal. Julie insisted, with heel
and rein and voice. Bonnie backed up. Julie spoke
sharply and dug in. Bonnie reared and plunged, as
the girl clung to her seat with sudden astonishment;
only once before had the filly reared under her, and
then there had been a terrifying raccoon involved.

Rearing again, Bonnie almost dislodged Julie. Dismayed, the girl knew that a third such attempt might
bring the horse crashing over on top of her, and was
ready to slide off and throw herself out of the way; but
Bonnie danced sideways and turned her tail to the gate,
and Julie allowed her to jig away. She halted her after a
few steps. Bonnie stood, blowing and tossing her head.

Monty was beside her. "You stuck with her fine," he
said, his voice shaking. "Julie, she's *afraid* of the gate."

"I know. And her such a perfect lady about it, before," said Julie, somewhat breathless. "It must be
that last race again. She remembers that it all started in
the gate. The poor thing thinks that *I'm* going to whack
her when she comes out of it!"

Monty said, very upset, "Even if you get your
license, it won't do any good if Bonnie's going to be a
problem in the gate."

"I know. What shall we do?"

"I—well, I'll rest her for a day. Then Sunday we can
try again." He was silent, chewing his lip and watching
Bonnie. "All we can do in the meantime is follow
Stash's system, and think good thoughts."

A man who had been leaning on the rail walked over to them. He introduced himself as an assistant starter. "That filly's entered in the Forget-Me-Not, isn't she? Isn't that Sunbonnet?"

"Yes," said Monty, "why?"

"Well," said the man in a stern, warning sort of tone, "she won't be allowed to start unless she's been okayed out of the gate. And from that performance, I'd almost give you odds that she won't be approved."

"We've never had any trouble with her before. I think she's having a bad day," said Monty.

"Didn't she dump her jockey a while back?"

Monty and Julie reluctantly admitted that Bonnie had, indeed, dropped Beau Watkins over the side.

"We've been told to keep an eye on her. I'd say she was a pretty dubious entry right now."

They jogged back to the shed row, as gloomy as a couple of paraders when the light shower turns into a cloudburst.

Chapter IX

Saturday brought a rash of minor ailments and be-havior problems, the kind of day a trainer dreads, especially when he is far from home and has a score of horses to care for. The four Deepwater people climbed into their beds about midnight, and crawled out again at dawn, groaning; but Sunday proved as good as Saturday had been miserable, and everything cleared up as though it had never existed. Not one of the twenty beasts showed a symptom of illness or irrita-bility. They were exercised in threes all morning long, and every one ran like a winner. Monty shook his head, muttering something about dark clouds and silver linings.

"Julie," he said, over lunch, "you take the afternoon off, all of it if necessary, and spend it with Bonnie at the gate. I'm going to give you Dan to work with, too. No, wait a minute: Bonnie's fondest of Beau, so long as he stays out of the saddle. I'll give you Beau. Don't take any chances, but be firm with her. And good luck."

If Bonnie didn't shape up today, he thought, there'd be nothing to do but withdraw her from the Forget-Me-Not. But there was no use in telling that to Julie now. It would only worry her.

So, laden with so many treats, so many gumdrops and apples and carrots and sugar lumps that Beau swore they were both walking bowlegged, the girl and the jockey left the stable at one thirty with Bonnie in tow, and headed for the starting gate. And, uncounted ages later—that is, about a quarter to five—they returned, with almost all the treats now inside the horse, and a couple of grins stamped indelibly on two tired faces.

Monty, who had been too busy to check on their progress, took a long look at them. "She made it," he said.

"She didn't want to come home," said Beau. "She wanted to stay in the gate."

"It's her chosen spot," added Julie. "She'll break cleanly, 'cause she knows it's the thing to do, but she wants to go right back and get into that nice cozy box immediately."

Monty felt as though he were drawing his first deep breath in a week. "How did you *do* it?" he demanded, sitting down on a bucket.

"Rewards, psychology, and infinite patience," said Julie.

"And love," said Beau. "The love of a good woman for a fine horse."

"Seriously, how did you do it?"

Julie wiped her wet and dirty face with an even dirtier hand. "Ve-er-ry slowly," she said. "Honest. We started at the beginning, as if she'd never seen a gate in her life, and took her through the whole bit by inches, cramming delicacies down her throat practically without stopping. If she doesn't have an ache in her stomach tonight, I'll be amazed. And we just kept doing it over and over, giving her a cram course I guess you'd call it, and telling her how marvelous she was, and after a while she loosened up and kind of smiled at us, so I got on her and there was no problem at all. And that man was there too, the assistant starter, you know, and when we'd got her to dash out of the gate for about the twentieth time he came over and said she evidently *had* been having a bad day on Friday, and she looked great now. So we did it twice more just to show the world we could, and we walked home."

"Limped home," said Beau.

"Oozed home," said Julie. "I can't remember being this tired since final exams last May!"

"She didn't give you any trouble?" asked Monty, weak with relief.

"Not a bit. But we acted—oh, for hours—as though she would. I tell you, Monty, we went through the motions so carefully you'd have thought we were all moving underwater."

"I never heard a horse flattered so much," added Beau. "I bet Man O' War never heard so much praise in a month. And you know, Mr. Monty, she understood every word. You could tell by her expression."

"And she came through for you," said Monty. "Now if we can just get her to overcome her aversion to having a man ride her . . ."

"If we approach the problem the same way," said Julie, "it shouldn't take us more than twenty-eight months. Really, I don't know *how* we can apply the same technique to her when she's running. Beau and I racked our brains about it, when we saw she was coming around to our side in the disagreement about the starting gate. We didn't come up with anything."

"But with the gate thing okay," said Beau, "if Julie can just ride her in the Forget-Me-Not, we're home and dry, like they say."

So now all they were waiting for was an answer on Julie's license.

The wait was not a long one. On Tuesday, just two days later, she received a letter from the Florida Racing Commission. She opened it with hands that were suddenly sprouting five thumbs apiece.

It was brief to the point of curtness. Her application was denied, on the basis of a lack of experience.

Julie wailed loudly. "Talk about your vicious circles! How can I get the experience they demand, if they won't let me ride?"

"Doggoned if I know," said Monty sympathetically. "We'll frame an appeal, Julie. We'll say in a nice way that they at least have to see you ride before they pass judgment."

"Now?"

"Now."

This time the answer was even more prompt. But this time, it was Yes. The stewards and representatives of the racing commission would watch her ride—out of the starting gate and a full mile and an eighth—this Saturday morning.

"Oh wow," said Julie thankfully, and went off to work horses with a much lighter heart.

Saturday was a fine day (Julie was growing used to fine days, and feared that she was being spoiled for northern weather), with a light soft breeze and plenty of sun. Bonnie was plainly feeling her best and most cooperative. Julie had enough butterflies inside not to be able to eat breakfast, but when it was time to get in the saddle and walk her filly toward the gate, she found herself moving steadily and without panic. "Because I *have* to be good," she whispered to Bonnie, "I simply *have* to be."

And she was, and so was Bonnie. Dan Gibson rode with her on the mare Fancy, and Beau on Curious Cottabus; all three broke cleanly and strong from the starting gate and swept around the track nearly head and head until the last couple of furlongs, when Fancy was distanced, the other two coming to an almost photofinish. Bonnie, the girl thought, had been beaten by a few inches—but she had not been running at her top speed, and Beau said that the Cottabus had.

The stewards and racing-commission people went away, their heads together, and Monty was optimistic. But again, when the answer came, it was an unqualified denial of her request for a jockey's license.

"That isn't fair!" Julie cried. "I didn't foul up at anything, and neither did Bonnie! They're discriminating!"

"Sure looks that way," nodded Beau lugubriously.

"I don't know what to do next," Monty admitted. "I suppose we just have to try matching you two again," he told Beau, jerking his thumb at the sweating filly. "We'll do it Tuesday morning at dawn."

"I'm game if she is," said Beau. "We've gotten to be awful close friends by now, 'bout as close as possible unless I was to wake her up in the middle of the night with more gumdrops."

Late Monday night Rollin Tolkov jetted into town. He had returned unexpectedly from Europe and instead of going from New York to Deepwater Farm, had come to where his trainer and some of his finest horses were staying. Sitting in Monty's room at the Martingale motel, with all the others asleep and only Monty aware that he was at Hialeah, Mr. T relaxed and smiled at the young man over the rim of his second cup of coffee. "It's five o'clock tomorrow morning as far as my European-adjusted system is concerned, and I'm about ready to fall asleep on your rug, but I want to hear about the horses first."

"Well, there's nothing much new since my last report," said Monty. "The Cottabus looks like a sure winner in the—"

"Sunbonnet. Tell me about her." Mr. T's smile faded. "The last I heard, to refresh your memory, she'd thrown young Watkins and the track was threatening to withdraw her from the race."

Monty told him briefly of Bonnie's trouble at the starting gate and of how that had been cured. He summarized the story of Julie's application for a jockey's license and the refusal of the authorities to grant her one. Mr. T held up a hand.

"That horse has got to run. Somehow we have to keep her in the lineup. And she ought to win. I feel certain she has the stuff to win."

"So do I—if she can conquer whatever's keeping her from running with a man in the saddle. Julie's being very brave and sensible about the whole thing, but it'll break her heart if Bonnie turns out to have been spoiled by one stupid jockey in one unnecessary race."

"And I'd go a long way round the barn to keep Julie's heart intact, as you know," said Tolkov. "But Monty, there's a lot more at stake here than Miss Jefferson's feelings. Principally, there's a prodigious amount of money, which will be made from the sale of Bonnie's foals after she retires from racing. I'll get my investment back with interest, and Julie will become a pretty well-to-do young lady. *Provided* that Bonnie retires with the track record that her breeding, and her brief career so far, indicate she ought to achieve." He poured himself another cup, and took off his Parisian necktie. "I'm not implying that money is more important than Julie's emotions, you know that. But winning races is how a stable earns its keep. It's how a great horse justifies its breeding. It's what allows us, the men who love horses and racing, to stay in the business."

"Right," agreed Monty. "That's why I'm working for you—to win races."

"Bonnie's won a single race that counts. She's already in her third year of life. She's way behind where she ought to be. She *must* run in the Forget-Me-Not, and finish in the money."

Monty nodded. He was not aware that he was sitting on the very edge of his chair and clutching his knees as though he intended to pulverize them.

"So you tell me now how you intend to make sure that Bonnie wins next month."

Monty blinked. "Well, if Julie can't ride her, it has to be Beau. Tomorrow morning I'm trying him again in a workout. I've spoken to Leon Pitt and Stash Watkins about the problem, and they agree that everything known to man is being tried with the filly. If she chucks Beau tomorrow—"

"Then we'll simply have to try something new and unheard of." Mr. T suddenly grinned. "Do I sound like the heartless, heavy-handed employer?"

"No, like a man who wants a horse to win."

"Also you're getting your first taste of Tolkov's Way. Which is to try everything possible, and then go on and try everything *im*possible."

"I'm stuck for impossible ideas, I admit," said Monty.

"I don't have any myself. But that's why I hire good men. Like you."

They regarded each other quizzically. "Right," said Monty.

"Right," said Mr. T.

Chapter X

A blue and gold dawn found all of them at the rail:
Rollin Tolkov, Rand Jefferson, Monty, and Dan Gibson. The first two had met at breakfast and liked each
other on sight. They were talking antiques now, a subject that Rand knew backwards and Mr. T was much
intrigued by. "I have this biscuit porcelain clock," Mr.
T was saying excitedly, "with a Vulliamy movement—"

"That'd be early nineteenth century," said Rand.

"Yes, I'd say 1805 or so. The ormolu decorations—"

"I'd give something to see that."

"You'll see it for nothing, by George! I'll be here for
the Forget-Me-Not, of course, and then you and I will
go up to Deepwater and spend a day with my clocks.
I have a coaching clock that may be by Daniel Quare;
I'd like your opinion on it."

"You make my mouth water," said Rand happily.
"And it's pleasant to hear, for the first time in weeks,
about something besides horses."

"I imagine it is. But speaking of horses—"

"Ah, yes," said Rand, "here she comes." He
glanced sideways at Mr. T. "Our little girl."

"She's quite a person, Rand."

"She is that. I'm grateful that she's working for
you."

"So am I," said Mr. T. "In addition to being
thoroughly honest and the hardest worker at Deepwater Farm, she's a ray of sunshine on any given dark
day."

"Unless she's fretting over her filly."

"Well," said Mr. T, watching the two horses and riders approach down the track at a comfortable jog, "I think a lot of that was caused by the newness of that big bay critter in her life. Monty tells me she stews less than he does these days."

Monty, hearing his name, came over to them. "You'll notice that Beau's on Bonnie," he told them, "and Julie's right beside them on Gramarye. I'm trying a new strategy. They're going to work head and head all the way, if Bonnie will run at all for Beau; I hope that Julie being right there will give the filly confidence. And she and Beau are getting along beautifully at a trot, you can see."

They were. You would never have believed that this calm, big horse had ever deposited Beau in the dirt except by purest accident. They drew to the starting gate and entered it without trouble. Dan Gibson had climbed the tower and now he pushed the button that rang the bell and flipped open the doors. The two burst out as one.

To the seven-eighths pole and around the clubhouse turn, the run was uneventful. Bonnie was on the rail, with Gramarye at her right, and the pace was good but not demanding. Then at the three-quarter pole, there was a noticeable change; as Monty watched them tensely through his field glasses, they both lengthened their stride, the powerful hindquarters driving them forward like a pair of glorious running-machines, and as Bonnie's naturally long stride took her for a moment to the forefront, she appeared to falter. Monty kept his eyes glued on her. She fell back a little, Gramarye now half a head in advance, and Monty would have laid odds on it that Bonnie was ready to wheel and bolt once more. Julie pulled her mount in quickly, watching the filly constantly, and Beau was talking into her ear and then she had settled down and the two were head and head and breezing down the backstretch and around the far turn.

Bonnie was running very well, though certainly not at her top speed. Beau was holding her in. But now at the top of the stretch Gramarye was tiring, for even Bonnie's second-best pace was too much for him. Julie

was urging him on and Beau was now more obviously
holding Bonnie in. Still, halfway down the homestretch
Gramarye fell behind, and Bonnie was suddenly a
length ahead.

That was the end for her. Finding herself out front
and alone, she did not try to throw her rider, but she
simply quit running. Julie pulled in Gramarye, and the
two of them crossed the finish line at an easy, rather
sloppy canter. Gramarye was plainly tired, and Bonnie
seemed confused and—if Monty was reading her correctly—a little frightened.

"That's it!" he said aloud.

"What's it?" asked Mr. Tolkov.

"That bat-happy jockey never began to hit her until
she was leading the field! They were at the quarter
pole, and two lengths ahead, when he went to the bat!
It isn't men she's afraid of—at least, she isn't afraid of
Beau—it's being alone in the lead. She associates heading the pack with being whipped."

Mr. T whistled quietly. "If you can't cure that, she'll
never win a race again, son."

"I'll cure her. There has to be a way to erase that
bad experience from her mind. I'll do it some way!"
He turned to face the older man. "But I'll bet you that
she'd come around to staying in the lead if Julie was
riding her. I think she'd run anywhere for Julie."

"Well, work on that, then. Let Julie ride her with two
or three others—"

"That's what I had in mind. Let her win a few
'races' with Julie up. And if she will, if she'll do that,
then maybe she'll come around to winning under
Beau." His face, which had been full of excitement and
hope, clouded. *"Maybe,"* he said.

"I'm all too aware of how hard it is to get into a
horse's brain and predict what it will do in any given
situation," said Mr. T. "But this looks like the best
chance to me. Meanwhile, I'm going to get in touch
with my lawyers at once, and have them contest the
denial of Julie's jockey license on the grounds of dis-
crimination against her because she happens to be a girl.
I see no other reason they could have had to refuse her.

And the best chance Bonnie has in the Forget-Me-Not is with Julie riding her."

"Do you really think they can change the commission's mind?" asked Rand.

"If they can't, nobody can," said Mr. T grimly.

Julie and Beau had now ridden over to the rail where the three were standing. Monty briefly told them what he and Mr. T had decided was wrong, and what they intended to do about it. Then the girl and Beau walked their mounts back to the shed row. They gave them to a couple of exercise boys to be cooled out. On their way into the stable to collect three of the Deepwater horses to be worked next, they passed a tall brown man in a Stetson who was just going out into the morning sunshine. Julie stopped dead.

"Beau! Do you know who that was?" she gasped, a hand at her lips. "That was the man who tried to claim Bonnie!"

"I know. Rodinbaugh. I've been seein' him around the track for a week or better. Don't know why he's hanging out here, he's got no job with anybody."

"He's still after Bonnie!"

"Why you say that, Julie?"

"I *know* it! Did you see the way he looked at me? He hates me, because I got her back and exposed his scheme, and he knows how much she's worth and—"

"Now, Julie, have some sense," Beau counseled her soberly, sounding almost exactly like his father. "Sure, he prob'ly doesn't exactly *like* you, but there's no way in this world that he can get Bonnie! Why," he paused and searched his memory for some famous thief, "old Jesse James himself couldn't lift a horse out of Hialeah! How's that no-account Rodinbaugh goin' to do it? No way."

Julie, remembering the night when Alex Homer had intended to shoot her lovely filly, said, "Then he'll try to hurt her."

"Why would he want to do that? He's not a crazy man. Just maybe a mite crooked."

"He—he could hide behind a corkscrew," said Julie vehemently. "I'll run get Monty."

"You won't either do any such a thing," said Beau.

"Mr. Monty's already talked to the stewards, and to Mr. Lillie at Kandahar, too; and if they couldn't do anything about Rodinbaugh bein' here, then there can't be any danger. And all we saw him do was to walk out of the barn! That's nothin' to raise a fuss about. Man has a perfect right to walk out of a barn."

She pulled at her lower lip dubiously. At last she said, "You're right. He just scares me. I admit it, Beau, he does scare me. But he can't hurt her, can he?"

"He's done all the harm he'll ever do to her, just lettin' that fool jockey ride her that time. You forget him, Julie."

"Right. Let's get the horses, Monty's waiting."

But Rodinbaugh's image, dark and wicked, stayed in her mind all the rest of the morning.

Things at the track ran smoothly while Mr. T's lawyers prepared their case. Time, though, was growing short, and now there were only nine days left before the Forget-Me-Not. They would have entered Bonnie in another race, as a final preparation for the stake; but since she obviously wouldn't run well for Beau, and since Julie couldn't ride her until something happened to reverse the denial of her application, there was no use in trying that. They exercised her in the mornings, and hoped for the best.

This particular morning, the filly had done very well indeed. With Julie riding her, she had slightly outrun the Cottabus, staying half a length ahead down the entire homestretch. Although she still would not go to her full drive unless she had competition that she could see beside her, she was slowly improving, Julie recognized, and perhaps by the time of the race she would have recovered her natural exuberance, untainted by bad memories.

As Julie was cooling her out, however—it had been the final workout of the morning, and the girl could do this as part of her regular chores—she noticed that the filly was acting a little strangely. At first Julie could not have said precisely what was different about her. She certainly was not going lame, or itching or having an attack of nerves or any of the other ailments that are common enough for a high-bred, high-strung animal. She was simply not quite her normal self. As soon as the girl realized that *something* was wrong, she riveted her gaze on Bonnie and watched everything about her: gait, the motions of her head and ears, the rippling of the skin on her withers and flanks, even the expression of her great brown eyes. She could not determine what was changed from the filly's usually behavior.

Perhaps nothing was. When she was watered off and cooled out, Julie walked her back to the stable, still observing her closely; nothing. But something. Just a shade of an alteration in her movements. Nothing to put one's finger on—but *something*.

When you know a horse well enough, when you have lived closely with it for a long while, then you can sense when everything is not quite right. The horse acts . . . well, a little "funny." Julie stalled her and leaned on the door for a few minutes, watching her. Then she went off to lunch, thinking hard.

She ate in a little restaurant near the track with her father and Monty. Halfway through the meal, Rand said, "You're a long way off, Julie."

"Hmm? Oh," said Julie, blinking, "I'm sorry! What were you saying?"

"Nothing important. What's on your mind?"

"Bonnie. She's not quite herself."

"In what way, honey?"

"I don't know." She told them what she'd noticed at the cooling-out, which, when put into words, was positively nothing. But the uneasy feeling remained.

"Let's take a look at her as soon as we've eaten," suggested Monty. Julie was not a girl who made up things to worry about; her fears were usually based on pretty solid grounds. Monty thought back. "She hasn't been worked too hard, that's for sure."

"Or too little?" asked Rand.

"No," Julie answered him, "this wasn't too much energy or anything like that. More like—well, maybe too little. As if she was a shade off her feed, you know?"

"Has she been?"

"Eats like a horse," said Julie, not meaning to joke about it, though both the men chuckled.

The three of them went to the shed row. Bonnie, in her stall, did not greet them as was her custom, but moved restlessly from side to side, stamped a few times, then turned her head to look at her flank, with an expression that would have been comical had it not indicated something serious, which occurred to all three humans at the same moment.

"This girl has colic," said Rand. Monty nodded.

"I'll get the medicine," said Julie, and her father, turning to her, saw that she had gone pale under her tan. There are three kinds of colic, and all three can be fatal.

He went into the stall and examined Bonnie closely. She was not sweating yet, which meant that she was not in much pain: enough pain from any cause will always make a horse sweat. Again she gazed back inquiringly at her flank.

"I don't like it, Monty."

"No. Needless to say," Monty muttered, "she's been getting an absolutely perfect diet. Salt block there, clean hay, plenty of water every day, no exercise on a full stomach—"

"Like a swollen leg, though," Rand growled back, as both of them looked her over from stem to stern, "you can seldom say just *what* caused it. Maybe it's a mild case."

"We'll see."

Julie came back, hurrying, with the bottle of colic medicine, some warm water, and a dose syringe. She mixed a couple of ounces of the remedy in an equal amount of water drew it into the syringe and expertly shot it down the filly's throat. She noted the time. In another twenty minutes Bonnie would get the second dose.

"Now we'll walk her," said Monty. "I'll take first turn." And in relays they walked her, through the early afternoon sunshine, around and around until Rand's back began to tire; this was after Bonnie's third dose of the ginger-cardamon-aromatic medicine. By now the filly was obviously nervous and in enough pain and excitement to make her sweat. She was walking now with a halting, careful movement quite unlike her usual motion. She was holding her beautiful head low and pausing often to stamp heavily with her forefeet.

Monty sent Dan Gibson for the track veterinarian. Rand, looking bleak, excused himself and went to the motel to rest his back. Julie and Monty walked the horse back and forth, back and forth, silent with worry.

The vet came, a short, middle-aged man with marvelous hands and a love for animals that showed in every word and touch. He gave her a tranquilizer and examined her in the stall. He was with her for what seemed hours to Julie; actually it was nearly half an hour. Then he said grimly, "I've done everything I can for now. I've given her a massive dose of tranquilizer to keep her from rolling and kicking; with luck it'll knock her out enough to do that, but you've got to stick right here and prevent her thrashing as much as you can. You know that. I'll be back in a few hours. Meanwhile, stay close to her and hang tough." He went away, his fear only partially concealed from them.

Julie looked at the big horse. Bonnie's breathing was quick and shallow, and her head drooped low. "She won't die."

"Not if we can help it," said Monty.

"She won't die," Julie repeated. It was not a question, said for reassurance. It was a flat statement. Julie's bonnie girl was not to end her life in pain on a stall floor in Florida before she had hardly begun her career. That was that.

Monty prayed that Julie Jefferson was right.

He went to the nearest phone, which was well out of the stable area, and called Rand. He brought him up to date. Rand said, "Look, son, don't worry. And I'll do what I can out here." He hung up. Monty stared at the phone a moment; it had been a curious thing to say. What could Rand do? Monty wondered.

Then he returned to the stable.

Julie, kneeling beside Bonnie, who was lying down on her side with all four legs thrust straight out away from her, said distractedly, "Could it have been all those

treats we gave her, Beau and I, when we were training
her to the gate again?"

"No! That was days and days ago. This is something
recent. We don't know what it could be. It doesn't
matter, anyway. She——"

"Could it be Rodinbaugh? Could be have given her
something that would make her sick?"

"Don't even think about him, Julie. He hasn't been
near her."

"We saw him coming out of the stable a few days
ago. He just *glared* at me."

"Because a fellow glares at you, it doesn't mean he's
going to poison your horse." Monty repeated essentially
what Beau had said to Julie on that occasion, that she
was still affected by the fright that the two criminals
had given her last year. "You know how easily a
Thoroughbred can get colic, Julie."

"Yes, I know. I'm just scared. But she'll be all right."

Without warning, Bonnie hurled herself from one
side to the other, kicking her legs and twisting to get
rid of the pain that, however dulled by the medicines,
was still tormenting her. A horse cannot vomit, and
poor Bonnie, baffled and frightened, was trying to make
herself feel better in the only way she knew.

It was a terribly dangerous method. One really
violent roll could twist an intestine, peritonitis would
follow, and then Bonnie would be finished. Monty
hurried into the stall and between them they managed
to keep her quiet. But her eyes rolled at them and she
did not understand why they, her friends, should prevent her from easing the pain inside her.

"Poor baby," Julie said, half-choked, "poor baby
Bonnie."

Under the satiny reddish-brown hide, the filly's
stomach was bloated and taut, and she glistened with
sweat. Now and then she shuddered as the pain
gripped her. The short, quick breathing was distressing
to hear.

After a short time she stopped trying to roll and lay
quiet, gazing dumbly at the wall of the cubicle, her
eyes gone vacant. Julie bent over the long head. "Oh,
Monty, is she——"

"The tranquilizer's working, I think." If she hasn't twisted a gut, he thought. If only she hasn't. "Maybe she'll rest a while now," he said, ashamed that his voice trembled.

Julie sat down by Bonnie's head and smoothed the big jaw with the tips of her fingers.

Chapter XI

By early evening the vet had seen her twice more, and had done all he could to ease her pain. With colic, little more could be accomplished than this; the actual cure would either happen or it would not, and meantime they could only keep her calm and as free of pain as possible, and try to prevent her from rolling in the deadly dangerous fashion that any horse will adopt to relieve the agony.

"Where's Dad, I wonder?" Julie said aloud, when the vet had gone. "It isn't like him to drop out of sight for so long when an animal's sick."

"I'll call him," said Monty. "Look, can I bring back something for you to eat?"

"I couldn't swallow a bite, thanks."

"Me neither." He went up to the gatekeeper's room and phoned the motel. The desk clerk rang Rand's room, and after half a dozen rings came back on the line.

"Mr. Jefferson hasn't come back yet."

"But he went there a long time ago. I talked to him there at about two o'clock."

"But he left shortly after that. I saw him go. He drove away and hasn't returned. I'm sorry."

"Okay, thank you." Monty rang off. He rubbed his cheek, thinking. Where in the world . . .

He walked back slowly to the shed row. Beau had now joined Julie in the filly's stall. Monty said to them, "Rand isn't at home."

"But where *is* he?" demanded Julie.

"I don't know. Maybe he's at dinner."

"I wish Mr. T hadn't gone back to Deepwater."

"He knows a lot less about horses than you do, Julie. Even Leon Pitt couldn't help us now."

"I know. I'm just so tired and scared, I wish everybody was here to hold my hand, that's all," said the girl wearily.

"Go lie down someplace and sleep a while. I'll call you if there's any change."

"Oh, no! I couldn't." She looked from Monty to Beau and down at Bonnie. "Oh, I'm being a pain. I guess I will." She left the stall, wandered down the row a short distance, discovered some bales of straw, and curled up on top of them. In two minutes she was sound asleep.

"Beau," said Monty, when he was sure that she was out of earshot, "it isn't like Rand Jefferson to vanish without a word. I only hope his back isn't acting up so badly that he had to go to a hospital. That's the only reason I can imagine why he'd drop out of sight. He wouldn't want to disturb Julie when the filly's sick."

"He'd have let one of us know, Mr. Monty. At least me or Dan, if he couldn't contact you."

"Yes. Well, there's enough to upset us here, without giving a perfectly responsible grown man another thought," said Monty, and endeavored to put this into practice. "How does she look to you, Beau?"

The jockey turned his dark eyes up to the other man's. "She looks bad, Mr. Monty," he said. "She looks about as bad as she can be."

After Monty had called Rand at two that afternoon, Rand had sat on his bed thinking hard for a couple of minutes. Then he had put in a call to the St. Clair Farm in Ohio.

"Stash? Rand Jefferson. We got troubles." Rapidly he told the groom of Bonnie's illness. "Do you remember a talk we had, you and I, a long time ago, when we were sitting up guarding Bonnie, when Matthews was out to nail her? About various home remedies we'd used on animals that were sick?"

"Sure. Lily leaves and all that."

"You told me about a way of relieving the colic, a

pretty unorthodox way, that you used to use in bad cases. Back before there were so many vets around."

"I recollect that, yes, sir."

"Stash, I doubt very much that a modern veterinarian is going to use that method—"

Stash chuckled humorlessly. "I'd say you were safe enough in that doubt."

"But if she doesn't improve, it looks to me as if by tonight that method is the only thing that won't have been tried. And you *did* have some success with it."

"In the old days. Yes. I haven't tried it in longer'n I want to calculate. It's a truly last-ditch operation, I tell you that. Why, you want me to come down there and try it?"

"Could you? Could you leave St. Clair at such short notice?"

"Mr. Everett, he sets a large store by you and Julie and that filly, all three. He won't give me no harassment. And you got to remember, Mr. Jefferson, it's winter up here and duties ain't so thick an' fast as they come in the summertime. I can get away." Stash chuckled again, this time sounding more like himself. "I'll just apply for a slightly advanced piece of my vacation, which I never took last year anyway, now I think about it. You want me to come, then, for sure?"

"I do. Maybe it'll be a wasted trip—maybe the filly will be better when you get here. But we can't take the chance. We have to at least prepare to try everything. And after all, this technique of yours is still used routinely on cattle, Stash."

"Yeah, but a cattle has four stomachs, and a horse got one. It makes a difference."

"If she's still down when you arrive, it will be time for desperate measures."

"Right. Now first thing of all, you got to c'llect me the instrumentation I need for it. Not much at St. Clair I could borrow in the way of what we need. Got a pencil? All right, you c'llect me these: a long, hollow needle, hypo-what's-it, you know what I mean?"

"Hypodermic needle, like the ones they use to perform spinal taps on people," said Rand.

"That's it. Better get two. An' alcohol an' cotton 'case

there's none handy. You also c'llect me about eight
hundred pounds of good luck. And I'll be there as fast
as an airplane can get me there."

"I'll be at the airport to meet you. If I'm not, call
Monty at Hialeah Park—ask for the gate—and we'll
get you out there."

"I'm on my way," said Stash, and clicked off. Rand,
feeling a little better already, went out to the car and
headed for the nearest drugstore.

After more explaining about the reason for his need
then he had expected, he was told that no drugstore
within fifty miles would carry such a needle in stock.
He thought briefly of going to a hospital and obtaining
one; the thought of what arguments he would have to
use *there* was enough to send him searching for another
drugstore. The manager there was more helpful but
just as pessimistic. "No, sir, you couldn't find one of
those, short of a surgical supply house."

"Well, could you direct me to one?" said Rand
earnestly.

"Give you the address of the one we use. It's the
nearest." The manager wrote the name and address on
an index card. "Driving? Well, you'll find it's just a
hundred and sixty-seven miles from our front door.
Good luck."

"Thanks," said Rand, and went out to the car as
briskly as his sore back would allow. He headed north,
nudging the speed limit.

With the customary traffic problems, plus a horrible
twenty minutes during which he ran out of gas, stood by
the side of the road flagging motorists, reached a gas
station and bought two gallons and hitchhiked back to
the car, then returned to the station and filled her up;
and finally a now-frantic search for the street on which
the surgical supply house was located, which included
passing it three times because its window had recently
been broken and the new one had not yet been painted
with the firm's name—Rand had consumed more than
three hours before he stood, rather pale and perspiry as
he fought the aching pain in his overworked back, and
explained his need to the man in charge.

"I hope you don't intend to do a spinal tap on somebody," said the man severely.

"No, no, no," said Rand, and sketched out the problem with Bonnie.

"Oh. You want to trocarize a horse."

"I wasn't sure the operation had a name. I won't be doing it myself; a top groom is coming down from Ohio to do it. He's experienced."

"Hope he knows what he's doing. That's a very, very risky thing to do to a horse. You take a cow, now—"

"Pardon me, but I'm in a terrible hurry. I have to get back to Hialeah."

"Sure. Well, let me see some identification, and have your name and address on this card." Rand did so. The man scratched his chin. "All right. Just wait here." He was gone several minutes. Rand mopped his face and thought about calling the track to find out how Bonnie was, but decided against it. The man came back. "Here it is."

Rand paid him. "Many thanks," he said, slightly relieved now that the apparatus was actually in his hand.

"Hey," said the man, as Rand turned toward the door. He grinned. "Best of luck, Mr. Jefferson."

"I'll drop you a card and tell you how it works," said Rand.

"I'd appreciate that."

He got into the car again and sat for a moment breathing deeply and flexing his back muscles to ease them. Then he headed out for the Hialeah airport.

It was past seven when he parked the car and walked, stiff and weary, into the terminal. Two slow glances revealed that Stash was not there. Rand, after some reasonable persuasion, discovered that the groom had not been on either of the flights that had arrived within the last six hours from the Columbus airport, where Stash would have gone to catch his plane. The next flight was due in a little more than an hour. It did not amaze Rand unduly when the plane proved to be half an hour late. He stood up and hobbled to the gate when it was finally announced. In two minutes he was shaking Stash's powerful black hand.

"Sorry I'm late," said Stash, as they walked toward

the parking lot. "Two planes for Florida was full up. Had to fuss 'n' stew around the blame airport all afternoon. Got me a cancellation, last-minute, on this'n. Thought I never *would* get here by then. How's our fine filly?"

"I don't know, Stash. I've been gone since two o'clock. Had to travel about four hundred miles to get the needle."

"I been thinkin' good thoughts," said Stash mournfully. "But I sure do despise a bad case o' colic. Seen it carry off too many good horses."

They got into Rand's car. He turned the key and pressed his foot down and there was not a single murmur from the engine, not even a throttled grunt. He repeated the action three times before Stash said, "No good. Your battery's gone."

"Oh *no*," said Rand helplessly. This was just too much. "It's been acting perfectly okay."

"No earthly use in takin' chances, Mr. Rand. We gotta hedge our bets fierce. I'll rassle up somebody with a jumper, but meantime you hike on in to a phone and call Monty and have him come out here with another car," said Stash, taking charge instantly as he realized how very tired Julie's father was.

"Good thinking," said Rand. In a couple of minutes he was talking to the gatekeeper at the track. Swiftly he explained the situation; the man on duty said that he'd see Monty or Julie had the message at once. Rand hung up. "If I were a cussing man," he said aloud, "I do believe that at this particular moment, I'd cuss." Then he went back to the silent car.

Stash managed to find a man with a set of jump cables in his car, and after the usual backing up and fiddling with wires and clamps, they endeavored to start the battery. They failed. They gathered around and in the white glare of a couple of flashlights, prodded knowingly here and there. "Defunct," Stash muttered, "It is defunct."

The stranger said, "Look here, your terminal's gone. Corroded and then busted. Miracle it started for you at all."

"Right," said Stash. "We can clean her 'n' try again, but I think we need a new terminal."

This proved to be true. Rand snarled at himself for not taking better care of the car's internal workings; but of course they had all had a lot on their minds lately, and he had been too wobbly to do much tinkering or even checking-up. The stranger left, after assuring them that the nearest garage was four miles away and likely closed.

"Well, we just wait for Mr. Monty, then. You sit in the machine, and I'll walk around in a little circle and watch for him." Stash gently and firmly guided the exhausted convalescent into the front seat. Now he took time to examine the hypodermic, and nodded. "That's it. I can do the job with that. Hope I don't have to, though. Mighty dangerous. But . . . we'll see." He began to walk up and down before the car, squinting at every vehicle that entered the lot.

Time passed, as slowly as cold molasses poured from a small-mouthed jug.

Bonnie was lying on her side, no longer able to find the energy for walking or even standing. Occasionally a heaving shudder would run through her distended body. Her breathing was shallow and much too fast. She could not even struggle against the obvious pain that filled her, and the only sound she made was the short, sick panting. By the light of the single bulb that burned in the stall, Monty and Beau and Julie knelt by her head, trying desperately to reassure her by touch and soft word.

Monty never knew afterwards what had made him turn and look up, beyond the stall, at the man who stood in the aisle watching them. There had been no sound from him. Perhaps there are stares that can be subconsciously felt. He looked at the man blankly.

"I just heard," said Rodinbaugh. "I only heard about her now."

Chapter XII

It all happened so quickly that there was no order in it, movements and words piling atop one another with crazy haste.

Julie cried out, shrilly, hysterically, so keyed up from the long, anxious vigil that she could not control her voice, "Watch him, Monty, he's come to hurt her!" Beau said loudly, "Easy, Julie!" and Monty, reaching out from his squatting position to put a calming hand on her arm, overbalanced himself and fell back half sprawling on the straw. Julie bounced to her feet and staggered from the swiftness of her movement, and Beau caught at her to keep her from falling, all three of them suddenly bursting out with the part-word-part-noise cries that people make when they are badly startled. There was nothing in Rodinbaugh's abrupt appearance to cause panic, certainly; but Julie's yelp shook them all badly. Before they had got hold of themselves and stopped thrashing and shouting, Bonnie, dully frightened by the sounds and motions, kicked out her forelegs and raised her great head.

Her left hoof caught Monty flat on the right shoulder, in the instant of time during which he lay on his side in front of her. A sharp pain streaked through him and involuntarily he added a yell to the general hubbub.

Then Rodinbaugh was into the stall and, brushing aside the jockey and the girl, took Monty under the arms and hauled him away out of range of the deadly hoofs.

"What in thunder's wrong with you people?" growled the tall brown man, as he propped Monty against the wall. He began to unfasten Monty's shirt.

Julie made a supreme effort and managed to control herself. "I'm sorry," she said thinly, "you scared me."

"I'm a monster," growled Rodinbaugh. He pulled the shirt gently off Monty's shoulder. "Didn't break the skin, but she caught you a good one," he said. "Try moving the arm."

After a pause, Monty, white in the face, said, "I can't seem to feel it."

Rodinbaugh prodded expertly. He seemed to prod and squeeze forever. At last he said in his harsh voice, "Preliminary diagnosis, but don't count on it: I *don't* think it's broken. You're lucky if it isn't."

"Why can't I move it?" Monty demanded.

"A bang like that numbs every nerve it touches, sonny." He thumbed back his big hat, scowling. "Watkins," he said, without looking back at the two who stood behind him, "run for the vet. He's seen plenty of these. Best he looks it over before we try to dig up a doctor, at this hour."

"Yes, sir," said Beau, and vanished into the night.

Julie said huskily, "I apologize, Mr. Rodinbaugh. I'm—" and then could not find the right words.

"You're beat," Rodinbaugh said, flexing Monty's shoulder muscles carefully. "This horse must have been sick for most of the day, from the look of her, and I don't suppose you ate any dinner. You're on edge. That's all."

"Yes, but I—"

"Don't keep going on about it. I don't think there's any vast amount of damage. How's it feel?"

"Starting to hurt some more," said Monty between his teeth.

"Small wonder," said Rodinbaugh.

He turned to look at Bonnie. "Not much strength left in her," he said under his breath. Julie looked into his blue almost-white eyes and felt a coldness in the pit of her stomach, as though danger flashed at her across the eerily lighted stall. But he was helping. She tried to shrug off her ridiculous terror of him; she could not do it. He said, "I think we'll take you out of here, sonny. One invalid's enough to a cubicle." Then he picked Monty up and set him on his feet. "Shaky?" he said roughly.

"Well, yes," Monty admitted.

Rodinbaugh supported him across the stall and down the aisle to the bales where Julie had slept earlier. He made Monty sit on them. "Don't lie down, it'll feel better upright. Can you flex the fingers?" Monty tried and succeeded. "Good. Got some feeling in the arm now."

"Yes," said Monty, "and it's all bad."

"Thank your guardian angel she didn't catch you in the head." Rodinbaugh stood back, looking as tall as the ghost of Cole Younger in his vaguely western clothes and the big Stetson. He drew his brows together in a heavy frown and bared his teeth, thinking. Monty stared up at him. He looks like a hungry wolf, the young man thought; it isn't surprising that Julie's afraid of him. What's he bothering about me for?

"Where in blue tunket is that indescribable vet?" demanded Rodinbaugh.

"I'm sure I don't know," said Monty defensively.

"I wasn't asking *you*," said Rodinbaugh.

Julie came out of the filly's stall. "How is it, Monty?"

"Great," said Monty, wincing.

"I'll bet that's as satisfactory a kick as you've had all year," said Rodinbaugh. "Blast! I don't even have an aspirin on me. Sorry," he said, amazing Monty, who would as soon have expected sympathy from the stable goat.

A man whom they did not know came into the stable. "Anyone here named Everett or Jefferson?" he asked.

"I'm Julie Jefferson."

"Got a message for you. Your father and Stush or Stitch or somebody are at the airport—"

"Stash!" Julie exclaimed. "Dad must have called for him this afternoon!"

"And their car's dead," said the man. "They want someone to go and get them."

"Thanks," said Monty. He looked at the girl. "I can't drive in this condition, Julie. You'd better go."

"Dear Stash, he'll help her. Oh," said Julie blankly, "we don't have a car. Dad took it."

The veterinarian hustled in, followed by Beau. Rand and Stash were forgotten for the moment, while he made a careful examination of Monty's shoulder. Then he stood up and said, "I'm rather a specialist in horses, young fellow, and this is an unofficial verdict: I doubt very much that anything's broken. But you're going to see a people doctor right away." He gazed around at them all. "Did I hear it said that you don't have a car handy?"

"Mine's outside," said Rodinbaugh.

"That's all right, I'll take him. Let's move, lad," said the vet. "The sooner you have a little painkiller jabbed into you, the happier you're going to be."

"I can't leave Bonnie," said Monty. "She's bad." .

"Well, I've done everything in the book of modern medicine for her, and you aren't going to help her by holding her hoof," said the vet. "Come along. Miss Jefferson and Watkins here can nurse the poor critter as well as anyone at this stage."

"Will she get well?" Julie blurted at him.

"I don't know. Honestly, I don't know." He helped Monty off the bales and led him out. The man who had brought the message drifted away after them. Julie moved over close to Beau, feeling the dread of Rodinbaugh's presence; she was almost supernaturally frightened of him.

"I've got to get Stash and Dad," she said. "Oh, Beau, we don't even have a car here! What am I going to do?"

"You sayin' my pop's here with yours?" Beau asked, brightening.

"Yes, at the airport."

"That's wonderful! Pop's the only man that might help ol' Sunbonnet now. Though I don't know *how*," he said. "Look, you go and call for a taxi. That's the only way."

"Bounding bangtails!" shouted Rodinbaugh, so loudly and irritably that Julie actually shrank back from the noise. "What in the pink-eyed world is *wrong* with you Deepwater people? Didn't I just tell you that I have a car right outside?" He glared at Julie so hard that his eyes nearly crossed. "Come on, I'll get them for you. But you'll have to go along and identify them for me."

"I'll be p-perfectly happy to c-call a cab," said Julie.

"Look, little girl," said the tall brown man in a tone that could only be described as vicious, "I gather that you are scared silly of me. Well, that's what it is, silly. You have a dying horse in there, don't you realize that? I'd give an arm and a leg to help her, but I can't do as much as Doc Wilson can. I gather that young Watkins thinks his father might help her. At this point you have to snatch at any straw that floats along. Now, are you going to come with me, or do I carry you under my arm?"

Julie, now rather crowded back against the wall by the force of Rodinbaugh's bitter exasperation, attempted to answer him, and managed a squeak. Even in the midst of fear and worry, it embarrassed her that her vocal cords had failed her.

"Watkins, get in there and baby-sit that poor filly," said Rodinbaugh.

Beau looked at him levelly for a moment. Then he said, grinning, "You aren't so tough," and went into Bonnie's stall. "Go with him, Julie," he said over his shoulder.

"But!" Julie said, after several tries.

Rodinbaugh rolled up his cold, light eyes and regarded the ceiling as malevolently as though a piece of it had fallen on him. He said a couple of things in a voice so strangled that Julie could not understand them. Then he strode over to her, picked her up as if she had weighed eight pounds, slung her over one broad shoulder, and walked out into the night. She was too petrified to squirm. A long, low-slung automobile, as menacing-looking as he was, stood nearby. He carried her to it and opened the door and deposited her gently on the seat. He slammed the door and walked around to get in behind the wheel. Julie thought of bursting out and running for her life, but before she could gather her wits and energies, they had started.

And so, she and Rodinbaugh (*she and Rodinbaugh!*) drove off through the night on their way to the Hialeah airport.

Chapter XIII

In silence, surrounded by the powerful purring of the big engine, they covered the first mile or so. Then Rodinbaugh cleared his throat and said, "Do you honestly believe that I'm out to kidnap you and hold you for ransom?"

"No," said Julie. "Well, I don't quite believe it," she added honestly.

"But I scare you so much your mouth goes dry."

"Yes."

"Why?" he asked curiously, in his strange, coarse voice.

She thought hard. "Because you tried to s-steal Bonnie," she told him, "and you look so—"

"So mean and miserable," he said, and chuckled in his throat. "I know it."

She turned to look at his profile, flickering dark and bright as they passed various brilliant signs along the road. "No, so tough," she said. "Like a, I don't exactly know, like a . . ."

"A gunman." It was a flat statement, as though he had said, "I am a trainer of horses," no more, no less.

"That's it." She was startled at her own frankness. She realized abruptly that she was less afraid of him than she had been since that day in Jack Lillie's office.

"Kid, the only gun I ever owned in my life shot caps," he told her. "And that was thirty years ago."

They traveled on without speaking. At last she became aware that he was watching her, on and off, from the corner of his eye. When he saw that she knew it, he laughed. It was a chilling sort of laugh, but she was not shaken by it; she wondered why. Then she realized that this time she had heard it without the preconceived idea that he was menacing her, and had recognized something—it was the only way he *could* laugh, with a voice as growly and harsh as his. She said, "What's funny?"

"Me," he said, without further explanation. They had left another mile behind when he went on. "Has it dawned on you yet that you're perfectly safe with me, Miss Jefferson?"

"Yes. I apologize for the way I acted. But you did try to steal Bonnie—"

"To buy her. She was up for claims, you know. I only went about it the wrong way, because I hadn't any time and my boss was out of the country. Maybe I'll tell you about that. I think I probably will." He paused. "Sometimes when you say things out loud, you understand them better yourself."

"That's true." When he did not speak, she said, "What you said back there, about wanting to help Bonnie, you surprised me, because you really meant it."

"Sure I meant it. I'd do anything for a sick horse, anything. Horses are the best. If they hurt you, they only do it like she did with the Everett boy, accidentally, or because they're in the dark about what's happening. Horses aren't the smartest animals in the world. But till some fat-headed idiot spoils them, they're the sweetest."

"*I* think so too."

He looked over at her. "Do you know the story of Pegasus, the winged horse?"

Surprised, she said, "Of course."

"And what's-his-name, the fellow who wanted to catch him and tame him—"

"Bellerophon. He wanted to ride Pegasus against the Chimera, who was destroying the countryside." Julie could hardly believe that this conversation was happening. This terrible man who had tried to take Bonnie away from her, talking quietly about a Greek myth . . .

"At first, yes," Rodinbaugh said. "But when he was waiting by the spring for Pegasus to come and drink, he fell in love with that great marvelous beast, with the idea of it. It turned into a vigil of love. He'd never even seen it yet, but hearing about it and watching for it, he gradually came around to wanting Pegasus just to *know* him, instead of as a weapon against the demon. Did you ever fall in love with the idea of a horse, Miss Jefferson?"

"Not exactly. But I love Bonnie. You know that," she said.

"But in the abstract. With a horse you've never even seen. That's a thing to happen to you! Maybe it only happens if you live—if you live with dreams and horses instead of people. You get to wanting the one perfect horse, which doesn't exist. Then you hear of a horse that comes as close to the ideal as you'll ever know. And you have to have it. You'd do anything just to keep it with you, train it right, see that it's as happy and well taken care of as a horse can be." He broke off and laughed jarringly. "Get me!" he said, choking. "Going on like an adolescent. Sorry, kid."

"No you're not. I think it's a *beautiful* idea," said Julie.

He chuckled and was silent for so long that she thought he had decided not to speak again; she was sorry for that, because she was full of curiosity and a kind of admiration for a grown man who would say as much as he had on such a sentimental subject. Then he said, in an almost unintelligible growl, as if he were ashamed of his feelings, "How do you explain it? *I* don't know. Her bloodlines can't be beat, and when Dan talked about her I could almost see her, the grandest piece of horseflesh since Exterminator. But that wasn't all. She'd lived a regular odyssey, or maybe a fairy tale: the poor enchanted princess kidnapped and mistreated and almost killed. I wanted to make sure the rest of her life was perfect. I wanted to work with her and be with her. . . . I was sure she was the perfect horse I'd been looking for. I guess I never gave much of a thought to the girl who'd saved her. Except that you were a *girl*, for Pete's sake, and how would you know what to do with a horse like that?"

"I have a lot of help," she said defensively.

"You don't need it. You're fine with her. I've watched you for weeks. But I didn't know that then, you see? All I knew was what Dan told me."

"Dan told you about her? Dan Gibson, Monty's assistant?"

He turned to gaze at her for an instant. "Then you don't know."

"No. What?"

"I'm Dan's uncle."

"Oh! But I didn't even know Dan knew her story," said Julie.

"He got most of it from Alex Homer. He worked for Homer, you know, when Homer was Tolkov's trainer. He heard Homer was in jail, and he'd never liked him much, but he figured he ought to go and see him, cheer the poor guy up. And Homer told him all about Sunbonnet, because by then, with his pal Matthews spouting off the whole story to anyone who'd listen, Homer had nothing to lose, see? So Dan naturally told me about the horse by then, working with her at Deepwater. He didn't figure it for a secret."

"It wasn't, really. We just hadn't told many people about her yet. Then that's why Dan's so nervous lately," she said. "He thought we'd find out and fire him."

"And he's been worried about me. Thinks I won't find another job in racing. But I will, kid," said Rodinbaugh harshly. "It's my life."

"I'm sure you will," she told him soberly.

"Besides Homer bragging about how he's almost got his hands on a million dollars' worth of filly," Rodinbaugh went on, "Dan heard bits and pieces of the bad time she'd been through, from you and young Everett."

"I remember that," Julie said slowly. "We told him about how I found her in Sam Spire's horrible yard. And he heard who she really was from Homer. I understand it all now."

"No. You've got no idea what went on in my head when I saw her in the paddock that day and realized that *my* horse was up for sale in a claiming race for twenty thousand, a price I could afford." He bent over the wheel and glared ahead down the road, evidently seeing it all again in memory. "I was knocked on my

ear. A Bold Ruler filly, that some little girl had probably been going to turn into a saddle pony, right in my
hand. *All that horse.* The horse I'd been dreaming
about."

"I was *not* going to turn her into a saddle pony!"

"I know, blast it, I know. But I didn't know then, and
the thought of it had been driving me straight up a lot of
walls. I'd been combing my brains for weeks to think of
a way to get hold of her. But here she was for sale. I
didn't know the ins and outs of why she was, not till
afterwards when Dan told me. So here was a horse that
my boss, Jonas Black, would have bought like a shot if
he'd been there and known about her. He was out of the
country and I only had a few minutes. Why was she in
that race? *I* didn't care. I would have bought her, by
then, if she'd been lame!" He brooded for a moment.
"I don't think I spent any time speculating about why
she was up for that low a price. Because it didn't matter.
She was. And I was there. It was fate. I went and put in
a claim. I was half out of my skull."

When the next silence had stretched out to an un-
comfortable length, Julie said, "You claimed her for
Mr. Black, hoping you could explain to him that you
wanted her so badly, and hadn't been able to get in
touch with him—"

"Yes. It didn't seem crooked to me. Sunbonnet's for
sale. Technically, I can only bid for her if my boss
wants her. But I'm dead certain he'll want her when he
knows about her. And if he doesn't—and I was hoping
he wouldn't—then I'll buy her from him. Either way,
she's mine, because I'm his trainer, and I'll have the
training and tending of her for the rest of her life." He
coughed, perhaps with embarrassment. "Maybe in the
back of my head is the notion that I won't try to convince him of how great she potentially is. Maybe I'll
admit it's me that wants her so badly. So I go right
ahead and do the first crooked thing I ever did in my
life," he finished quietly.

Half an hour before, Julie would not have accepted
that statement if it had been handed to her by the spirit
of George Washington. Now she believed it without
question. Rodinbaugh, this strange, forbidding man,

was by his own admission a kindred spirit, a person who lived for horses in the same sentimental, whole-hearted fashion that she herself did. You had to believe in that sort of man.

"But you didn't think of it as dishonest," she said.

"Right. I was only cutting a corner or two. I just went up and put in my claim. Look, if I'd seen you with her before that, I don't think I'd have done it. How was I to know how close you and she were? She was for *sale,* after all. It's just since I came down to Hialeah and watched you together that it's dawned on me. You're the right one to own her. I know how much you went through for her, how you even risked your life for her. So the setup's okay with me the way it stands. If I can't have her, and I can't, then she has to belong to you." He glanced at her again. "I didn't have any inkling of that, back at Kandahar. I'm sorry I caused you so much worry. I've been working myself up to tell you that for days." He paused and then said in a bitter voice, "I don't apologize easily."

"But you do it awfully well," Julie said warmly. "I'm not mad at you any longer about it, Mr. Rodin-baugh."

"Or scared of me?" he demanded, biting off his words as if they had been slivers from a block of ice.

She thought. "No. Not a bit. You're a nice man."

At that he whooped. "I'm positive that nobody ever called me that before," he said, "not *ever.*"

"That's a sad thing, because I think you are."

"Under the rough exterior, a heart of gold," he barked, half-laughing. "No, Miss Jefferson, only with horses. I never bother much with people."

"Don't you like people?" she asked.

"They don't like me. Don't think I'm whining about that," he said, waving his hand in the darkness and sounding very angry. "It's pure-and-simple my own fault. But I don't care, really. When you've done such a thorough job on yourself as I have, you may reach a point where you realize you've botched up your life, but by then you can't do anything about it, and it doesn't matter anyway."

Julie, with a flash of inspiration and no reticence any

longer concerning this tall rough man who seemed so sad to her, said, "I think you were a lonely little boy."

"No," he said, "not in the sense you mean it. I was alone, but there were plenty of horses, and I never minded. And you're trying to pump me. That's impertinent," he said. "Little children shouldn't pry."

"I wasn't prying!"

"Yes you were. And feeling sorry for me, and *that's* impertinent too."

"Oh, you're impossible," said Julie irritably.

"You're blame right I'm impossible."

After a while she said, "I'm not a little child. And you can't be nearly as bad as you make out, because you're not a crook."

"Do you think an honest man can't be a holy fright?" he shouted at her. "Haven't you been ready to screech for help every time you saw me?"

"I thought you were after Bonnie."

"And I have a smile that would scare off a shark, and a voice you could use to slice cold iron. And I dress like an 1885 gunslinger, and carry my hand over an invisible holster, and prowl instead of walk, and if you saw me when I wasn't frowning you'd believe that I'd just died."

"Not that bad," she protested.

"Sure, that bad. Don't I know myself? I *made* me," he told her. "I'm a perfect example of a self-constructed Frankenstein's monster, Old West style. Billowing curtains of flame!" he burst out, with his curiously antique style of expletive. "Why in blue tunket am I spilling my private soul to you? You're prying."

She didn't even answer that. The lights of the airport glowed palely white on the low clouds ahead of them. She watched him, and at last he said, speaking as though in a dream, "No. I know you aren't prying. I'm sorry. But we're both worried sick about that filly back yonder, with the colic destroying her. Let me teach you a moral lesson, while the fit's still on me and my tongue's loose. You deserve to know everything about the business, for being so pleasant with a guy who tried to take your horse away. Listen to me and learn."

"Learn what?"

"To be yourself." He sighed. "I had an uncle. Actually, a great-great uncle. A genuine gunman. He's in the history books. His name was the same as mine. He left the States in 1872, bound for Africa, after he'd made this country too warm for himself, and nobody knows what ever happened to him. But my grandfather started to tell me about him the first day I could totter around on my own feet. Like any kid would, I developed a case of hero-worship for the old thug. I thought, Man, how great to be like that, with everybody making room for you and calling you 'Sir.' That's fine for a day or two when you're a tad playing Billy the Kid on a lonesome ranch with no playmates, but if you keep it up until it gets hold of you, and year in, year out you're a bad guy standing alone against the world—"

After a long stillness, he went on. "Even anyone as young as you can figure what'll happen. You turn into a bad guy. It's a miracle that I didn't. I had a good mother and father, though, and almost no other influences till I was grown. They educated me themselves. So I'm—I'm not such a terror. Honest."

"I know that," said Julie.

"But outside, which is where people look, I'm the meanest, orneriest horsethief who ever walked. I played the silly part for so long . . ."

"Out of loneliness," Julie supplied.

"And hero-worship. It's pretty exhilarating to be related to some bigger-than-life wild man out of the history books. Anyway, when I was old enough to really know better, I'd stuck myself with this pose, this snarl and grin and prowl. I looked silly in normal clothes, so I didn't wear 'em. If I tried to talk gentle, with my voice and the way I'd always used it, I sounded like a halfwit. Why bother trying to change? I was me, what I'd made me." He gestured vaguely in the air. "If you learn from that to always be yourself, not somebody you *wish* you were, I'll have done my good deed for the year. But the way I see you, you know that already."

"I used to try and imitate actresses," said Julie thoughtfully.

"Fun for a few minutes, but miserable if you keep at it till it's second nature."

He sounded so suddenly mournful that it would have been laughable, had he not been so serious. "I'll remember," Julie said, and knew that she would. Poor Rodinbaugh, she thought; he certainly was a frightening example of how mannerisms take root. She resolved never again to pretend she was anyone but Julie Jefferson.

"I'll tell you something else you've taught me," she said, as they slowed for the turnoff to the airport. "That's not to go around judging people by what they look like. Why, I was more terrified of you than I ever was of the real, dangerous criminals I'd met! And you're as nice as can be."

"I set you off on that track by trying to take your horse away," he said gruffly.

"But I understand that now. And I spent more energy being scared of you than I did over things that were real, like Bonnie's not running right."

"My fault," he growled. "Well, here's the parking lot. Watch out for them. Say, kid," he added, looking sideways at her under the shadow of his big hat, "nobody needs to know what we've been talking about."

"Of course not. That's private."

"You're okay," said Rodinbaugh, delivering the two words as if they had been a witch's curse.

"There they are. There's Stash, and Dad in the car."

"They better know something that'll help our filly," said Rodinbaugh grimly, "or I'll have them toasted for breakfast." Then he laughed, horribly. Perhaps only Julie would have known that he was making a joke, and that the laughter was directed entirely at himself.

Chapter XIV

If Rand Jefferson and Stash Watkins were astonished to find themselves being chauffeured by the man who had tried to separate Bonnie from Julie, they disguised the fact admirably. They listened as the girl brought them up to date on the filly's condition. Then Rodinbaugh asked Stash what he thought he could do for her.

"Little operation we used to use in the old, old days," said Stash.

"He's going to trocarize her, if it seems necessary," Rand said.

Rodinbaugh whistled. "That's a last-ditch forlorn hope," he said. "I used that just once, on a horse in the same condition. The horse would have died anyhow."

"But it didn't?" Julie said breathlessly.

"It did," said Rodinbaugh flatly.

"There's no need to frighten Julie, is there?" asked Rand a little angrily.

Rodinbaugh shook his head. "Your little girl needn't be protected from the cold facts of horse life and death," he said, expertly passing two cars and dodging back into line. "She may be fourteen or so, but she's grown up when it comes to Sunbonnet."

"I'm seventeen!" snapped Julie.

"How was I to know? I don't go around figuring out kids' ages."

"Sorry," said Julie.

He glanced over at her and smiled briefly. "Don't sweat it," he said.

"I won't." She moved nearer to him and said under

114

her breath, "I've been thinking. I'm going to talk to Mr. T about you. I bet he can help you get back into racing somehow."

"Who's he?"

"Rollin Tolkov."

Rodinbaugh whistled. "That's a man I'd like to have on my side."

"If you don't mind me telling him the facts about your claim, I think he'll help. He's a very understanding man."

"I don't mind," said Rodinbaugh. He smiled in the gloom of the now-dark road. "I won't be getting my trainer's license back, you know, Miss Jefferson, but any job with a racing stable is all right, and a hundred times better than a job where there aren't any horses."

"Please," she said, "everyone in racing calls me Julie."

"Okay, Julie," he said, and throwing back his head, gave his biting laugh. In the back, Rand and Stash stared at each other in wonder. What sort of tough character had their little girl gotten herself mixed up with *now?*

They reached the track shortly, and then the shed row. They all dashed into the stable, even Rand with his bad back going at full speed. Beau was alone with Bonnie, who glistened black with the sweat of pain and did not even lift her head to look at them.

"Mr. Monty hasn't come back yet," said Beau. "Hi, Pop."

"Hi, Beau. How's our big old filly?"

"She hurts."

"Sure she does. That's a shabby, dismal, exasperatin' ailment to have, that colic." Stash bent and examined the horse. "Yep. Hmm. Julie, what's the vet say?"

"That he doesn't know. He's done everything he can."

"Then, is it all right with you if I try what I came down here for? It's dangerous. Like your friend there says, it's the last ditch."

"What if you don't?"

"Then I'm afraid she isn't gonna make it," he said gently.

"Go ahead. I understand." Julie clenched her fists behind her back until the nails hurt her palms. "Go on, please, Stash."

"We have to get her up on her feet and keep her standin' the best way we can. It isn't gonna be easy. She wants to keep lyin' down. But it'll take me a minute or so to find the place, and when I got it located, I have to stick this needle right into her side and let out that air that's painin' her so bad. She's gonna fight you then—you can imagine why—but you have to keep her up." He looked at Rand. "You better get outside, 'cause you're too weak after this day to help any."

Rand nodded and went into the aisle. Stash motioned Julie back against the wall. He said to Rodinbaugh, "You care to help?" and Rodinbaugh snapped, "Try to prevent me," and then the two of them with young Beau were shoving and prying and grunting and coaxing and shouting at Bonnie to force her to her feet. The filly grunted in dull surprise and put her head flat on the floor with stubborn determination. "Have to wallop her," said Stash, and to Julie's horror they all three began beating her with loud slaps of their open hands.

"It's all right, honey," said Rand, who was leaning over the half-door. "Sometimes it's necessary. They won't hurt her."

"I know," said Julie, trembling, "It's just so awful to see her like this. It makes me realize how bad she is."

Somehow they got her off the floor and standing, shaking and rolling her filmed eyes back at them. "Beau, take her head," Stash commanded. "You stand here and hang on when she explodes," he told Rodinbaugh. "Now I find that place."

He probed along her side as Bonnie, doggedly perseverant in the matter of lying down, kept trying to buckle at the knees. It was more difficult to keep her upright than it had been to raise her. But Stash, calm and masterly in his movements, felt and felt until he was as certain as he could be that he had found the spot he wanted. Then he reached into his hip pocket, pulled out the box, opened it with the fingers of his right hand while keeping his left on the swollen side of the horse, extracted the long needle and dropped the box. He squinted hard at the needle.

Julie held her breath and shook all over with sympathetic dread.

With a single thrust, as graceful and economical as a surgeon's, Stash buried the needle in the dark, wet body.

Bonnie's eyes fairly popped out of her head as she bounded forward against the restraining hands of Beau and Rodinbaugh, her hoofs banging and sliding on the floor. Through the big hollow needle, a great *whooosh* of air escaped from within her. It seemed to Julie that it would never stop.

And then it had stopped, and poor Bonnie, like a deflated balloon, stood miserably quiet with her head hanging low, fresh sweat pouring down her back and her heaving sides, trembling terribly and panting as though she had no air in her body at all.

Rodinbaugh said, "Man, that was fine. That was truly fine."

"Yeah, good work, Pop," said Beau proudly.

The three of them solemnly shook hands all round.

"Now we wait," said Stash. "I guess everybody better go outside 'cept me. I'll help her ease down if she don't feel like standin' any longer."

"Did—did it work?" asked Julie.

"It worked."

"Will she be all right?"

"Nobody can say that yet, Julie," said Stash. He began, easily and soothingly, with murmured endearments, to dry the horse off to some degree.

"But most of the pain's gone," said Rodinbaugh, taking her by the arm and leading her into the aisle. "She has a lot better chance now. That's a good man, that Stash."

"Right," said Julie.

They all watched Bonnie from outside the stall. Soon she emitted a sigh and lay down, with Stash helping. Stash sat down on the straw beside her. Monty and the veterinarian, Doc Wilson, came into the stable. Monty wore his right arm in a sling.

"Oh, Monty!" said Julie, stricken with remorse; she had totally forgotten his injury. "Is it broken?"

"X-rays say no. But the doctor says it's going to look like an Arizona sunset before I can use it again. How's Bonnie?"

Julie told them what had happened. Wilson went in and shook Stash's hand. "That's a thing I wouldn't have tried myself," he said, "but I'm mighty glad you did." He examined Bonnie. "All you can do is wait and watch now."

Rand Jefferson, pale with fatigue, said to the girl, "Julie, you know how much I want to watch with you, but I feel like a large, badly rotted tooth. I have to go to bed."

"Of course, Dad. I'll drive you—oh, the car's at the airport!"

"I'll take you to the motel," said Rodinbaugh. He looked at Julie. "Kid, if I bring back some Chinese dinner or hamburgers or something, will you eat it? Growing children oughtn't to go so long without food, or their bones will soften."

"You," she said to him, shaking her head, "you're incorrigible. I'll eat a plastic carton of grass if you can find one." She reached far up and kissed him on the cheek. (Monty gaped at this, and felt distinctly faint.) "Thanks so much for all your help," she said, "you old gunman."

No one else knew why the tall menacing man went out laughing in a most horrifying manner. But when they had arrived at the Martingale, after a silent drive, Rand put out his hand and said, "Blessed if I can imagine what all's happened today, sir, but any friend of my daughter's is a friend of mine."

"Shake," said Rodinbaugh, and did his best to smile like a person instead of a shark.

They all ate until they squeaked, as Beau said; then they sat around on bales of straw and waited. It was a long, long night. Gradually Bonnie began to show signs of being comfortable. At last, when earliest dawn was touching the earth beyond the big open doors, she snuffled at the hot bran mash that Stash made her, and dipped her nose into the metal feed manger and ate. Stash stared at Julie and slowly smiled wide.

"Can't guarantee that she'll be chipper enough to run in the Forget-Me-Not," he said quietly, "but I'll tell you this, Julie: she's gonna get better."

"Oh, Stash!" said Julie, and broke into dry, thankful sobs.

"Now I'll sit with her and see she has everything she wants, and the rest of you get some sleep," Stash ordered. Monty, Beau, and Rodinbaugh left the stable amid a profusion of thanks and mutual congratulations; but Julie curled up in a corner of Bonnie's stall and fell asleep to the rhythm of the big filly's normal, peaceful breathing.

Chapter XV

By noon the Deepwater clan and its cohorts had risen, yawned, eaten a late breakfast, and gathered at the stable. Bonnie was looking bewildered, but it was evident that she was not in pain any longer. Stash and Rand held a consultation about her with Monty. Together they worked out their plan: a special vitamin diet and feeding schedule that they hoped would bring her back into condition by the time of the stake.

"It's touch and go," said Monty, "but maybe we'll make it. We have to try, anyway. Mr. T says she's to win that race, and if it's possible in any way, she'll do it. This is the first big thing Mr. T's asked from me."

Coincidentally, at this moment a message arrived from the gatekeeper's room that Mr. Tolkov was on the phone for Monty. He and Rand got into the car, which had been retrieved from the airport after receiving what Stash called a battery-terminal transplant, and rolled off while Julie fussed lovingly over Bonnie.

"Hello, sir," said Monty into the telephone.

"Good news, young fellow," said Mr. T's jolly tones. "We've won. Julie will have her jockey's license in two days."

"Oh, wow," said Monty, "I can hardly believe it."

"How are the horses and the crew?"

"Oh, just fine, sir. Bonnie——" He was about to give his employer a briefing on Bonnie's illness, but Rand, to whom this was obvious, waved his hands and frowned and shook his head. Monty stumbled over a few random words and said Bonnie was perfect in the gate and they hoped, et cetera. Mr. T gave an audible beam into the phone and hung up. Monty said, "But he ought to—"

"No, no need to worry him now. We aren't keeping it from him, exactly, but it's part of an employee's job to absorb the minor shocks and only pass along the large ones. If she can't run, that'll be a large one. If she can, you'll have worried him for nothing."

"Besides," said Monty, "he might have wanted to cancel the entry."

"Exactly. Because you haven't worked for him long enough for him to trust your judgment implicitly in the matter of a very valuable horse. *We* know we'll run her only if she's perfectly fit. He might not feel justified in trusting our judgment." He got up and they walked to the door. "If it's necessary, we'll cancel her at the very last minute."

"Okay. I'm game. I guess Julie will be, too."

"Julie, son, is just glad her filly's alive. She'll trust you in matters like this. Now let's go tell her she's going to be a jockey." He slapped his thigh. "My little girl a jockey," he said, awed. "Wonders never do cease, do they?"

Monty thought of Julie giving the villain Rodinbaugh a kiss on the cheek. "They sure never do," he said vehemently.

It was two days before the Forget-Me-Not. After hand-walking Bonnie by the hour as her only form of exercise during four long days, it has seemed to them that the special diet was taking effect; so that for two days Julie had then jogged the filly, who perked up quite noticeably. As she appeared to be at least ninety-five percent of her normal exuberant self, she would be galloped lightly this morning and tomorrow morning. Then, provided that she kept on improving, they would run her despite her interrupted training schedule.

"Because I believe she can beat any horse in Florida right *now*," said Julie to her father. "Or maybe in the whole world!"

"I have little doubt on that matter myself, honey."

Beau brought in an early edition of the paper. "Hey, Julie, you made the front page," he shouted. They crowded around him as he waved it jubilantly. "You're famous," he told her.

"Julie always has been famous where it counts," said Stash severely, "at St. Clair Farm in Blankton, Ohio."

" 'Girl jockey to make debut in Forget-Me-Not,' " Julie read aloud.

"Out o' sight," said Beau. "Read on."

The story told in detail about Sunbonnet's past performance, mentioning the race in which she had been disqualified "for technical reasons"; but despite her two wins, she was considered to have little chance in the same class with the top two-year-olds of the past year. There was no mention of her background or breeding. The story concerned itself mainly with the novelty of a girl jockey.

"You feel novel, Julie?" asked Monty.

"I certainly don't," she said irritably. "Imagine them saying that Bonnie won't win! What do they know?"

"They wouldn't recognize a fine horse if it bit them," agreed Stash.

"Well, novelty," said Monty, "let's get out there and exercise horses, and earn our day's wages."

Julie saddled Bonnie, still grumbling behind her teeth, and went out to gallop her lightly against the top two Deepwater horses under Dan and Beau. Bonnie did beautifully. "Naturally," said Julie. She had crossed the finish line a good length ahead of Cottabus himself. Nor had she balked at finding herself in the lead. "Naturally," said Julie again, grinding her teeth. "What does a silly old newspaper know, anyway?"

Rodinbaugh, who had been leaning on the rail watching them run as usual, came over to her. "She's looking good," he said, resting his hand on Bonnie's neck. She nuzzled him affectionately.

Julie said, "Did you see the morning paper?"

"Stupid article," said Rodinbaugh.

Monty came over on Ginger. Of course Julie had long since told him as much of Rodinbaugh's story as was necessary to explain the claiming of Bonnie, but he still felt a twinge of jealousy every time he saw the man. Even though Julie informed him in no uncertain terms that she now considered Rodinbaugh as a sort of uncle, like Mr. T himself.

"What do you think her chances are?" he asked Rodinbaugh, half-unwillingly. The man's experience and knowledge meant something, though.

"I'll have money down on her, sonny," said Rodinbaugh.

"My name's Everett," said Monty.

"I know that, sonny."

Monty rode off abruptly. Julie said, "You shouldn't tease him. He doesn't understand you at all."

"Force of habit. I told you, I've been top gun too long."

"You can change. I want everybody to like you, as I do."

"You mean do a Scrooge? 'Ho ho,' said Scrooge, 'the spirits and Julie Jefferson have done it all in one night.'"

"You can do it. Try."

He looked up at her. "You might be amazed to know how hard I am trying," he growled. "Because it's not too bad, having someone like you treat me as if I wasn't going to give her a good backhand swat." He slapped Bonnie tenderly on the neck and walked away, his boots spurting up puffs of dust as he trod his unseen western boardwalk on his eternal way to the OK Corral.

And the next day, the day before the race, trouble broke over them from the most unexpected quarter.

Again Beau came shouting into the stable in the morning, waving a paper. This time it was the racing paper, and once more Julie had made the front page; but with a considerable difference.

An enthusiastic reporter, in digging out an expanded story about the "girl jockey," had traced most of Bonnie's history—which had not been a secret for some time, of course, and which now was given to the world almost in full. There was the truth about Bonnie's fabulous price at the Fasig-Tipton sales. There was the "alleged" plot of the "alleged" thieves to obtain her illegally; her final recovery and the jailing of said "alleged" crooks; and the full account of both her races, including the attempt of Rodinbaugh (who was, however, not named) to claim her fradulently, thus invalidating the filly's second win. There was a long paragraph about her sire and her dam and the marvelous lines of both. There was even a sentimentally written human-interest paragraph about the love and rapport between Sunbonnet and her owner, the young lady who could ride her, according to the reporter, so effortlessly that the two of them flying around the track looked like a senator.

"What?" said Stash blankly. "Who ever saw one o' them in a saddle?"

"I believe the writer meant 'centaur,' but was in a hurry," said Rand.

"What's this mean?" Julie asked them. "I don't like it much. It gives me a creepy feeling."

"You're just not used to publicity," Monty told her. "You'll have to get accustomed to it now, since you're going to be a famous jockey."

"And it means that the odds on Sunbonnet will become much more realistic," added Rand.

Julie continued, however, to feel uneasy; twice in two days she had seen her name and Bonnie's in print, and she could not get rid of a certain foreboding, as though she had been standing on a wide bare stage in the glare of an ominous spotlight.

"Oh," she told herself, "you're being impossible! Like some superstitious savage who's had his picture taken. You think part of yourself doesn't belong to you any more." Perhaps that was it: Bonnie, who had for so long been strictly hers, now seemed to belong to the world. "Well, don't be selfish about her, then," she said to herself severely, and went out to exercise the filly for the last time before the stake.

By chance, this was one of the rare days when all of them gathered to have lunch in the cafeteria at the same time: Julie, Monty, Rand, Stash, Beau, Dan, Irv Blaise, the Deepwater jockey who had just arrived to ride the Cottabus in one of the richer races upcoming, and even Rollin Tolkov, who had hurriedly wound up his business affairs in order to watch a few days of racing. They sat at a long table, and Rodinbaugh came in, dragged up a chair beside Julie, said, "Who's watching the store?" and sat down, to Monty's annoyance.

"Mr. T," Julie said, "this is my friend Mr. Rodinbaugh."

Mr. T, without a blink, shook hands with this old enemy and said heartily he was happy to meet him at last.

"He was terribly helpful when Bonnie had the colic," said Julie, which necessitated her telling the whole story to her boss, of the illness and the fear and Stash's doctoring and the filly's quick recovery. Conversation about this went on briskly during most of the meal. At one point, when Stash and Dan were arguing over the relative merits of two different aromatic colic medicines, with most of the others contributing on one side or the other, Julie told Mr. T in a whisper something of the spur-of-the-moment decision that had rushed Rodinbaugh into committing his first illegal act. "But I know him now, really well, and he's a *good* man," she finished, hoping that she'd paved the way for asking Mr. T to help him. "He's just gruff," she added, "but he loves horses and he's very good with them."

"And you want me to give him a job," said the other, smiling.

"Oh, no," Julie said, "you've given jobs to zillions of my friends already! Monty and Beau and Leon Pitt—"

"Not because they were friends of yours, though. Young Watkins was your only recommendation, as I recall, and I think he's worth his salt. I can't use anyone else at the moment, but I'll get acquainted with Mr. Rodinbaugh and see if I can't help him."

"You're super," said Julie gratefully.

Rodinbaugh bent forward; he had been talking in the general hubbub and had not heard them. "Julie," he said, "that blasted paper this morning. I think it's stirred something up."

"What?" asked Julie and Monty together.

"I'm not sure. But look over in the southeast corner where those four jocks are eating. They keep watching you. And I don't like their expressions."

As they saw the girl and several others turn to regard

them, the four jockeys carefully turned their faces blank and incurious. Julie said, "What could it be?"

"Don't know. But they aren't happy," said Rodinbaugh. "And by thunder, there's two more on the left, they're looking at you too."

"A cat may look at a king," said Monty, still touchy.

"And a jockey at a pretty girl," said Mr. T.

"I don't like it," growled Rodinbaugh, glowering around the huge room. "Something's up."

"Well, if it is, we'll find out, I'm sure," said Julie. She felt less comfortable than ever. I knew that story was bad news, she said to herself.

Just how bad, even the apprehensive Julie had no idea.

Chapter XVI

Rodinbaugh walked back to the shed row with them to look over Bonnie. Thus, there were four of them there—the tall brown man, Julie, Stash and Monty—when the deputation arrived.

They came in the wide doorway and walked back toward Bonnie's stall in a tight group, eight of them; small, lean men, looking nervous and determined. Stash saw them first and said quietly, "I think we got company." The four came out of the filly's cubicle and waited.

The jockeys stopped and the one in the lead cleared his throat and said, "We, ah, we want to ask you something."

Rodinbaugh moved a little ahead of the others and hooked his thumbs in his big, studded belt and said harshly, "Ask away."

"It's the girl we're talking to."

Rodinbaugh ran his eyes over them. He slid into his lifelong role. "And me," he said, because he did not like the look of them at all.

"Miss Jefferson," said the spokesman, "I'm Girty, I'm riding Regula Goodun in the Forget-Me-Not tomorrow. These are the other jockeys who're in it."

"Where's the other one?" demanded Rodinbaugh. "I count eight. Did Steuwe chicken out?"

"He didn't agree with us," said one of the men. "But we're a majority anyway."

"What is it?" Julie asked them, trembling slightly but not visibly.

"Well," said the one called Girty, "we don't want you to ride tomorrow."

"That's about it," said another.

"Spill it all," said Rodinbaugh. "You have your little piece memorized, trot it out."

"We ain't talkin' to *you*," said a jockey angrily. "We're talkin' to her."

Julie put a hand on Rodinbaugh's arm. "It's okay," she said, "this isn't a showdown."

"That's your opinion," gruffed Rodinbaugh; but he stepped back a pace.

"Now, look," said Girty in a reasonable tone, "we didn't mind riding against a girl, see? I mean, you got to move with the times, right? We didn't mind at all. You seem like a good kid."

"Thanks," said Julie, as he stopped and the silence seemed to expand to fill up the stable.

"But, you know, we thought you were just gonna be out there on that nobody filly with the bad reputation, see? And maybe we thought you were crazy to ride her in a big race, when she's been dumping Watkins all over the track for weeks, but that was your business."

"But on a horse that cost about half a million bucks," said a boy she knew, Maxwell, "that's different."

Rodinbaugh sputtered but did not interrupt as Girty went on. "We want to be reasonable, see? We don't object to riding against expensive stock. That's our profession. Especially when the horse is a pretty bad actor."

"She's not!" said Julie.

"Well, anyway. We got no complaints against competition. But when you're aboard, that makes a big difference. We aren't facing a normal thing there, do you see what I mean? We're facing a *team*. If what that piece in the paper says is true, we're ridin' against what we figure to be the wrong odds."

"And they're sprung on us too late," said Maxwell.

"Yeah. Maybe if we'd known all along we might feel different," said Girty, plainly trying to lean over backwards to be fair. "That article, though, if it's tellin' it like it is, it says nobody in the race is gonna have an even chance against the pair of you, see? You and that filly are—are just too much. It isn't *right*."

"The odds are unjustifiable," said a tiny, middle-aged jockey named Mo Harris. "You must see that. With you up, Sunbonnet is running way above her class."

"And that's how we all feel," said Maxwell.

"Except Steuwe," said Rodinbaugh with a sneer.

"Steuwe would ride against anything on four legs," said Girty.

"Or six, even," said someone else. "He's wild."

"Looks to me like he's the only one of the bunch with guts," said Rodinbaugh.

"Right on," said Monty, for the first time agreeing with Rodinbaugh.

"Now, be fair," Girty exclaimed. "We didn't come here to bully you, Miss Jefferson, honest. And it isn't any snap judgment. We've all been talkin' it over all morning. It's how we feel. Watkins on Sunbonnet, or Blaise up, even, that's one thing. You up, that's another. It's all too much and too late in the game then. We wouldn't ride against Shoemaker on a horse he'd lived with most of his life, see, and maybe this isn't quite the same, with you just getting your license and all, but it's too close to it for comfort. A Bold Ruler get, under the girl that raised her, well no thanks. Just plain no thanks."

"It really isn't fair odds," said Harris. "I'm on Blackbeard tomorrow, and he's the favorite, but he's not going out against the pair of you."

"You're only objecting to her because she's a girl and you can't get used to that idea," said Monty.

"No, I *told* you that isn't it. Maybe some of us aren't too happy about females invadin' the business," said Girty, "but like I told you, we know we gotta move with the times. No, I said my piece, and that's the way it is. We won't ride against a team like you two."

"So what do you intend to do?" asked Monty.

"If Miss Jefferson doesn't bow out, we'll boycott the race. She'll be riding against Steuwe on Red Unicorn, and it'll be a two-horse run."

"Boycott," said Julie. "Are you going to boycott Bonnie, too?"

"No. You put Watkins or even Blaise on her and we'll take her on."

"Julie," said Stash, regret in his voice, "there is somethin' in what these fellers say. The odds might be a mite unreasonable."

"I don't see that at all," said Monty, indignant. "They're paid to ride, they can't pick their competition."

"In this case, we're picking it," said Girty stubbornly, "and it isn't Miss Jefferson on her own mare."

"I ought to mop up the stable with the whole lot of you," Rodinbaugh rasped. "Bunch of lily-livered old ladies."

"What about it, Miss Jefferson?" said Maxwell.

Julie looked at the taut, restless group. "Can you wait until I talk to Mr. Tolkov? He has to have a say in the decision."

"Sure. You want me to go along?" asked Girty.

"That's all right, just tell me where I can find you."

"I'll be over by the starting gate in an hour. We'll give you till then. After that we go see the stewards."

Rodinbaugh growled something about quivery cowards. Julie said, "Thanks. I'll be there." The jockeys filed out, looking a little shamefaced.

"I'll sit with our filly," Stash told her. "They're good boys, mind you, Miss Julie, and they do have a point there. So you go talk to your boss."

Julie and Monty, with Rodinbaugh stalking beside them looking grim, found Tolkov in the complex of offices. He listened to them without comment. At last he sighed and said, "Maybe the subject's open for debate; maybe they've got the wind up and aren't being entirely fair about this. But I don't think you can change their minds this late in the game. I think it'll cost you Bonnie's chance of winning, but I have to say that you should bow in favor of Blaise or Watkins."

"I guess so," said Julie miserably. "Does that mean Bonnie should be withdrawn too?"

"No. Everett's brought me up to date on how she's running. I'd say she still has a good chance to come in in the money. Even if she won't go out in front of her competition, she's likely to place or show." He patted her hand. "I'm sorry, Julie. It's a rotten thing to happen to you."

"It wasn't that I had my heart set on being a jockey, Mr. T. It was only that I wanted her to win."

"I'm afraid this has cost her that chance. But let's give her a try at it, anyhow."

"I'll go see Reg Girty, then."

"Fine. Mr. Rodinbaugh, can I speak to you for a minute?" said Rollin Tolkov. The big man, surprised, nodded and sat down as Julie and Monty left them. "Jonas Black's here for the Forget-Me-Not," said the older man. "I had a talk with him about you. He says you're an excellent man with horses and he hated to lose you."

"That's decent of him," said Rodinbaugh.

"He wants to talk to you about a job. He can't take you on an anything resembling a trainer, mind, because you don't have a license. But if you're willing to serve as a kind of exercise boy and groom and what-have-you for him, in a year or so he'll throw all his weight in for you when you apply for another license."

Rodinbaugh stared at the floor. "I hardly know what to say."

"Just go tell him the whole truth. Julie confided some of it to me at lunch. I don't blame you, nor does Jo. You aren't the first honest man to lose his head at the prospect of a fortune."

Rodinbaugh looked up. "It wasn't the money," he said in his coarse voice, "it was the horse herself. It was never the money."

"I believe you. If Julie didn't think so, she'd never have told me that you were a really good man."

"She's a great kid."

"The best," said Mr. T. He held out his hand. "Good luck."

Rodinbaugh shook his hand hard. "I doubt if I can thank you enough," he said.

"You already have," said Mr. T.

Julie told the jockeys that she wouldn't be riding.

They were vaguely apologetic and a little confused;
they had never had to do anything like this before.
Julie smiled crookedly at Girty and said, "No hard
feelings," and took Monty back to the shed row.

"Who'll ride her?" she asked him.

"Irv is the better of the two, because he's had years
more experience."

"But she knows Beau best, and she loves him."

"Exactly. That's why I'm assigning her to Beau."

Beau took the news dubiously. "I know she'll run for
me, Mr. Monty, and she won't dump me 'cause she's
used to me now, but if she gets out in front, I'm scared
she'll just quit on me. And with nine other horses on
the track runnin' their hearts out, that could be real
bad. She might get run over. She might instigate a
jam-up that'd be bad news for a lot of men and
horses."

"I've thought of that. The only thing you can do is
keep her head and head with the other leaders until
the very last. Maybe you can manage that. If she takes
the lead and realizes she's alone it won't matter, if
she's already over the finish line."

"I'll do my best," said Beau.

"Right. Then tomorrow, you go to the post."

Beau went over and fed Bonnie a couple of gumdrops. "Well, princess," he said, smoothing her jaw
with the tips of his fingers, "it's you and me tomorrow. And all those others are out to beat you, you can
count on that. I hope you're going to be sensible. I
hope you remember we're friends." He looked into her
enormous, mild eyes. "Friends, Bonnie, old girl," he
said plaintively. "Just *please* don't forget that, will
you?"

Chapter XVII

Race day.

The infield was alive with flamingos, the stands were crowded with people. "The Star-Spangled Banner" had been played. The horses that were to run in the Forget-Me-Not stakes were in the paddock, all glistening in the sunlight. The multicolored silks of the jockeys shone here and there among them.

Bonnie had been pronounced in magnificent condition by every member of Tolkov's entourage. She had come from the shed row with head high and neck beautifully arched, stepped in her neat, proud way in among the other horses, and then, whether because of the crowds or band music or her own excitement, proceeded to get more nervous by the minute. Now she was stamping and nickering as Beau and Julie did their best to calm her.

"She's goin' to be okay," Beau kept saying, as he sweated in the vivid blue and white silks of Deepwater, "she'll be okay once she's out there."

"Sure she will," said Julie. She got up on Ginger, who would serve as lead pony for Bonnie in the parade to the post. "Easy, baby, easy." Bonnie looked up at her and threw her head sidelong and back, as if asking what under the warm afternoon sun Julie could be doing on *another* horse.

Post time sounded.

"Here we go," said Beau, grinning tightly at her.

She led Bonnie out of the paddock.

They had drawn Number Four position. They came

to the starting gate and Julie relinquished her, walking
Ginger sedately off the track.

Bonnie entered the stall coolly enough, then began
to back out of it. A handler ran over to her and did his
best, but she stubbornly refused to go all the way in.
Beau kept talking in a quiet, steady voice, saying anything that came into his head as he patted her neck
and tried to urge her forward. A kind of terror
flicked him, but he put it aside angrily, before it could
communicate itself to the horse. Bonnie fidgeted and
seemed about to rear under him. A second handler
joined the first; they pushed her by main force into
the stall and at last the box surrounded her. She
jiggled and fidgeted, breathing too heavily.

"Bonnie, you settle down and I'm gonna buy you a
regular mountain of gumdrops tonight," said Beau,
caressing her, looking to his right to see how many
horses were still to be enclosed by the great gate. Two
more only, and Bonnie evidently was the only nervous
starter. "You be a good horse or you'll bust Julie's
heart," said Beau, adjusting his posture to the correct
angles and unwittingly holding his breath. The horse
was telling him as plainly as though she were speaking
English that she didn't approve of being in there without Julie Jefferson.

The bell rang and the gates flew open and the vast
mob of spectators bellowed together in a surge of
sound, and nine horses leaped forward together onto
the track.

"Come on!" shouted Beau, dismayed.

Then Bonnie bunched herself and tensed the mighty
hindquarters and sprang out after them, four lengths
behind the pack, and the race was on.

She trailed them until they went into the first turn,
and then she had fallen naturally into her stride, the
formidable reach that was longer than the ordinary
and as relentless as her gallant heart, and she was
closing on the knot of horses, four of them, who were
in the rear. Beau, in the fraction of a second that is
all a jockey can take to decide such things, set her
straight into them, instead of taking the long way
round on the outside. She dove between the two in the

middle, as sure-footed as a young gazelle, and took the whole turn with delicate balance and fantastic drive, and at the three-quarter pole had gone ahead of them and was running sixth just behind and to the right of Blackbeard, the colt who was the favorite. A furlong later she had passed him too; Mo Harris was saving Blackbeard's great strength for the far turn, when he would make his move.

Julie, watching through Monty's field glasses, bounced up and down uncontrollably and shrieked. Stash Watkins pressed his palms together and thought positively. Rodinbaugh, chin cupped in one lean brown hand, scowled in a ferocious manner, and the people on either side of him moved away a little, as though he were a cannon preparing itself to go off with a roar. Rollin Talkov pounded Rand on the arm and shouted, "Look at her go! Just look at her go!"

A vast impersonal voice said over the almost intolerable howl of the crowded stands, "Number One, Red Unicorn, is first . . . then Number Three, Wendell C, and Number Six, Perfect Fool . . . and fourth is Number Five, Regula Goodun . . . Coming up very fast is Number Four, Sunbonnet, in the fifth position. . . ." And Julie didn't hear that the last five were Blackbeard, Half and Half, Indeterminate, Trinket, and Donegal, because Number Four was driving and gaining and simply *hurling* herself down the backstretch and carrying Julie's heart with her.

Beau pointed her head just to the right of Regula Goodun and the jockey, Girty, glanced over and his mouth fell open as Bonnie flew past on the outside like a swallow passing a pigeon.

" . . . And Sunbonnet is running fourth and still coming up fast on the outside. . . ."

Beau, poised with perfect balance in the short stirrups, took in the three horses ahead and planned his course for the far turn. For a breath he wondered whether Bonnie was not running too fast, expending her energy too soon; then he shook his head once and blinked and gave himself over entirely to the great filly's own marvelous judgment of her powers. *Run your own race, honey, you know what you can do better'n any of us.*

Not too many horses you can allow to do that, he said to himself, but this is sure one of 'em.

I trust you, Bonnie girl, I hope you trust me. All the way.

In the lead by two lengths, Red Unicorn, a flashy gray colt, with Steuwe, a wild, brave, and incredibly skillful jockey, in the saddle, went into the far turn along the inside rail. He had been in the lead all the way.

Harris made his move, and Blackbeard came up past Regula Goodun and took fifth and began to gain on the leaders.

Bonnie closed with Wendell C and Perfect Fool, and between them swept around the far turn; before the quarter pole she had distanced them and was running second.

On any other horse he had ever ridden, Beau would probably have now gone to the bat. With Bonnie, he did not dare it; at best, she would have been thrown off her stride—at worst, she would have bucked him onto the track. Hand firm and steady on the rein, he let her set her own pace with only the gentlest encouragement from her rider.

And she responded beautifully, closing the gap between herself and Red Unicorn, pounding around the bend and into the straightaway.

Behind her, the field was bunching again, as Blackbeard came abreast of the close-running Perfect Fool and Wendell C, and Trinket, a little marvel of a late-runner, passed Regula Goodun to take a tight sixth position. Girty now went to the bat and pressed forward. The last three were out of it, barring any spectacular moves; but for seven horses, from front nose to last croup spanning no more than half a dozen lengths, it was still anybody's race.

Bonnie, in this breathless thundering torrent of rocketing horseflesh and clicking, crashing steel plates and crouched intense men, pushed herself onward past the wet gray side and shoulder and head of Red Unicorn and was in the lead.

Beau Watkins commended himself to her care, and rode with a taut, but not tense, rein. Her nose was out in front and then she had half a length on the Unicorn and then, incredibly, solidly, she was one length in advance of him and still running at her best.

But she knew it. Suddenly she knew it, that there was no one beside her, that this was the homestretch where a horse who shoved itself into the lead earned a thrashing, that she was alone.

In the great clockwork stride, Beau could feel the first slight faltering. Bonnie began to swerve bit by bit toward the outside rail.

Red Unicorn and Blackbeard began to close the gap again. Regula Goodun roared past the others to make a solid fourth, with Girty's bat going methodically. Trinket went to the wide and pressed forward, going very hard indeed.

Beau leaned forward, thrust his small whip out so that Bonnie could see it, and dropped it with a quick flip of his fingers. *See, I'm not gonna touch you, sweet filly, I threw it away . . .*

Against the firm easy guiding of the reins, Bonnie deliberately swerved farther toward the outside, and now the rhythm of her stride was definitely broken.

The field had come up to her now.

Julie and Monty and Stash, at different points of vantage, each gasped as they saw the horse falter, and through their minds flashed almost identical imaginary pictures: of Beau fighting her, of Bonnie dumping Beau to be trampled by the other, bolting, becoming the focus of a bad pile-up.

Then Beau did a strange, an incomprehensibe thing. As they watched, astonished and fearful, they saw him stand up in his irons for a moment, exactly as though he was pulling up after a workout.

Bonnie, obviously confused, wavered badly in her stride. Red Unicorn and Blackbeard were definitely in the lead, and the tight pack of horses was surging around her. Then in an instant she seemed to take heart. Without a stumble she launched forward again into her invincible pace, and with magnificently controlled violence shot herself down the stretch at the finish line.

The stands shook with the howling of the crowd.

Like a beast on steel springs, the great filly passed Wendell C and Perfect Fool and closed with Regula Goodun and Trinket. Either the two leaders were tiring, or these three were running even harder; for the three swiftly gained and gained until all but neck and neck there were five of them sweeping forward, like the plunging vanguard of some wild fierce cavalry charge. And the finish line was there and they crossed it and a crash of sould went up that must have been heard in the West Indies.

The "photo" lights, dancing on the tote board, were really superfluous. Not a soul of all those thousands doubted that this had been the photo-finish of a lifetime.

Slowly, shakily, consumed with anxiousness and yet oddly satisfied already, the members of the Deepwater Farm contingent gathered from their various posts at a spot near the winner's circle. One by one the five horses who had led the others came there too. Stash was the first to reach up and shake his son's hand.

"Boy, you rode a nice race out there," he said solemnly.

Beau grinned down at him. "Rather hear that from you than get a slice of the purse," he said.

Monty clapped him on the knee. "You old Beau," he said, inarticulate with relief. "I had visions of you squashed out there, but—oh, man, you good old Beau!"

Beau dismounted. "This girl wouldn't let that happen," he said, patting Bonnie's steaming hide, from which the smell of hot horse was rising, pleasant in their nostrils.

"Who won?" asked Rand, coming up. "We couldn't decide."

"All we could be sure of was that Trinket was fifth," nodded Mr. T, shaking hands with Beau. "The other four were one grand blur. Incidentally," he added, "wherever you finished, lad, you've earned yourself a permanent job with me. That was a great race."

"She ran it," said Beau, mopping his face with his father's handkerchief. "I just sat there."

Julie said nothing, but embraced her Bonnie's neck, where the veins stood out beneath the sleek wet skin, and shed a few joyous tears onto her pride and delight, the best filly in the world.

"I think Red Unicorn won," said Monty. "Steuwe rode a terrific race."

"No," said Irv Blaise, "it was Harris on Blackbeard. I could see it plain as print from where I was." He kneaded Beau's arm. "Sorry, Beau. But you did ride her to a fare-thee-well."

"I agree with Monty," said Dan Gibson, who since his uncle's vindication was as consistently happy as a boy on holiday. "It was the Unicorn."

"My vote goes for Regula Goodun," said Stash. "I guess it depends on where you were standin', what you think. We'll find out quick, anyway."

"You're all wrong," said Beau. He reached out and touched the big bay, who looked back at him gravely. "We got there first, I *know* we did. See," he said, looking round at all of them, "she wanted to win. I told her we were friends, and I proved I was levelin' with her; and she said back, plain as day, that she was gonna win for me. So she went and did. That's *all*. She *won*."

"Likely we're all wrong, and it'll turn out to have been Donegal," said Monty. "Look, Beau, you did something that I don't understand at all. She was going to balk, and you—"

"I stood up." Beau chuckled. "I'll tell you about that as well as I can—say, where's Mr. Rodinbaugh? He ought to be here. It was something he said that occurred to me in the stretch when Bonnie was breakin' her stride. Where is he anyhow?"

"If I know him," said Monty, "he's waiting till the photos come through, and if they show Bonnie losing, he's going to start a terrible argument with the cameras."

"Right," said Dan, laughing.

"Why did you stand up?" asked Stash.

"Well, I'm not sure I can explain it, but it's got a lot to do with tellin' the truth," said Beau carefully. "I've never lied to Bonnie—never told her she had to do a thing that I wasn't certain she could do. I always tried to have things absolutely straightforward 'tween her and me. When that other jockey rode her and asked for her best, she gave it to him; only he didn't believe her. She was runnin' all out, but he hit her. She couldn't believe that I wouldn't do the same thing."

They all nodded as Beau paused. The tote board was still blinking its "photo" message. Julie and Bonnie were communing silently.

"When she first had her trouble in the gate, she was scared to believe anybody; but Julie showed her that it was all right, and Bonnie finally believed her. Today in the gate she wasn't sure she could do the same for me, and had a hard time decidin', but she took a chance and started to run. I let her know that it was her race all the way. She got to trusting me good and firm. She ran that whole race by herself, just askin' me to aim her at the right places. Which I did.

"Well, I thought we were home free, and then she found herself in front and she started to swerve. I didn't dare hit her, or she'd figure I'd been lying to her all along." He turned to Irv Blaise. "You know how your mind works out there? Specially when things are goin' tough?"

"Greased lightning," said Irv.

"Right on. I thought of what Mr. Rodinbaugh said to me this morning, when we were talkin' over Bonnie's problem. He said, 'When it comes right down to it, Watkins, you'll have to prove to her in any way you can, short of jumping out of the saddle, that she is the boss and that you are only along for the ride.' So then I thought, I'll show her the bat and I'll throw it away. 'Cause I wasn't gonna use the thing on her anyway, but she didn't know that. So I did.

"But Bonnie didn't understand that. Maybe she didn't even see it. And I thought again, *In any way, short of jumping off* . . . So I stood up. I just gave her the whole can o' saddle soap, and I said to her—in my head, I mean, there sure wasn't time out there to say *Boo* out loud to her—I said, 'Sunbonnet, if we've come this far and you still can't trust me, then I'm willing to pull up right now, see? Over to you.'"

"You took an awful chance," said Irv, shaking his head in wonder. "If she'd quit cold on you, there were three-four horses ready to pile up."

"I *knew* she'd go on," said Beau. "After all, if I didn't trust her, why would she go and trust *me?* I knew she'd think it over for a second and then she'd gamble on me."

He looked at the filly, a love in his eyes that could have been matched only by Julie's. "I wasn't off that leather two seconds before she understood what I was telling her. And she followed through. She said she was out to win that race for me. And she did." He stared around at them all. "And *that's* how I know we won," he said vehemently, "because she told me she would."

Nobody answered him. Several of them coughed with embarrassment, feeling positive that he was wrong in this sentimental idea. Their own eyes had assured them that Red Unicorn (or Blackbeard, or Regula Goodun, depending on where they had been standing) had most definitely come in first.

Then Julie said, "You'd better get up again now, Beau, they'll be wanting you in the winner's circle pretty soon," and Beau got into the saddle with a grin. Julie said to the others quietly, "He's right, you know. Bonnie won."

"Now, Julie," said her father carefully, "it's all very well to have faith in your horse, of course, but—"

"Julie," said Mr. T at the same time, "please don't get your hopes up too high, because I—"

"Julie," said Monty in agony, "you're building yourself up to a letdown that—"

"Julie," said Stash kindly, "it don't matter if she didn't—"

They were still saying all these things, with the best intentions in the world, when the tote board lit up to announce to a cheering crowd that Red Unicorn had placed and that Blackbeard, the favorite, had come in third by the barest whisker of length; but that first of all in this marvelous running of the Forget-Me-Not had been Sunbonnet, the great bay filly of Julie Jefferson.

More SIGNET Titles You Will Enjoy

☐ **EDGAR ALLAN by John Neufeld.** A penetrating novel that examines the problems that arise when a white middle-class family adopts a Black child.
(#P4113—60¢)

☐ **LISTEN TO THE SILENCE by David W. Elliott.** A total and unique experience—gripping, poignant, most often, shattering. A fourteen-year-old boy narrates the chronicle of events that lead him into, through, and out of an insane asylum. "Each page has the ring of unmistakable truth . . . a well-written, tour de force, another **Snake Pit** . . ."—**The New York Times Book Review.**
(#Q4513—95¢)

☐ **TRUE GRIT by Charles Portis.** A fourteen-year-old girl out to avenge her father's death during the 1870's and a mean and tough U.S. Marshal are the focal points of this brilliant piece of Americana. A major motion picture starring John Wayne and Glen Campbell.
(#Y5419—$1.25)

☐ **SOUTH TOWN by Lorenz Graham.** A realistic novel about a Black family in the South and one boy's ambition to become a doctor. (#P4409—60¢)

Other SIGNET Titles You Will Want to Read

Other SIGNET Titles You Will Enjoy

☐ **LAUGHING BOY by Oliver LaFarge.** The greatest novel yet written about the American Indian, this Pulitzer-prize winner has not been available in paperback for many years. It is, quite simply, the love story of Laughing Boy and Slim Girl—a beautifully written, poignant, moving account of an Indian marriage.
(#Q4769—95¢)

☐ **LOVE STORY by Erich Segal.** The story of love fought for, love won, and love lost. It is America's Romeo and Juliet and it is one of the world's most touching, poignant stories ever written. A major motion picture starring Ali McGraw and Ryan O'Neal. (#Q4414—95¢)

☐ **TO BE YOUNG, GIFTED AND BLACK by Lorraine Hansberry.** Adapted by Robert Nemiroff. By the author of **Raisin In the Sun,** here is Miss Hansberry's unique view of the human spirit, and her unwavering belief in the possibilities innate in human nature. "She knows more about the bloody world than any living playwright . . ." —Rex Reed (#Y5318—$1.25)

☐ **THE STORY OF SANDY by Susan Stanhope Wexler.** The moving true story of a foster parent's courageous fight for the sanity of a deeply disturbed little boy.
(#Q4517—95¢)
